SENSELESSNESS

Rainmaker Translations supports a series of books meant to encourage a lively reading experience of contemporary world literature drawn from diverse languages and cultures. Publication is assisted by grants from the Black Mountain Institute (blackmountaininstitute.org) at the University of Nevada, Las Vegas, an organization dedicated to promoting literary and cross-cultural dialogue around the world.

Horacio Castellanos Moya

SENSELESSNESS

TRANSLATED FROM THE SPANISH
BY KATHERINE SILVER

A NEW DIRECTIONS PAPERBOOK ORIGINAL

PUBLISHED BY ARRANGEMENT WITH HORACIO CASTELLANOS MOYA AND HIS AGENT THE RAY GUDE MERTIN AGENCY.

ORIGINALLY PUBLISHED BY TUSQUETS EDITORES IN 2004 AS *INSENTATEZ*.

PUBLISHER'S NOTE: GRATEFUL ACKNOWLEDGMENT IS MADE TO THE RAINMAKER TRANSLATION GRANT PROGRAM OF THE BLACK MOUNTAIN INSTITUTE FOR THEIR SUPPORT OF THIS BOOK.

AUTHOR'S NOTE: I WAS ABLE TO FINISH THIS TEXT THANKS TO THE GENEROUS SUPPORT OF ANA CAROLINA ALPÍREZ, GUILLERMO ESCALÓN, OTONIEL MARTÍNEZ, RODRIGO REY ROSA, AND EDELBERTO TORRES ESCOBAR.

TRANSLATOR'S NOTE: THE TRANSLATOR ACKNOWLEDGES THE ASSISTANCE OF THE BANFF INTERNATIONAL LITERARY TRANSLATION CENTRE AT THE BANFF CENTRE IN BANFF, ALBERTA, CANADA. TRANSLATION OF THIS BOOK WAS ALSO SUPPORTED BY A NATIONAL ENDOWMENT FOR THE ARTS FELLOWSHIP AND A PEN TRANSLATION FUND AWARD.

MANUFACTURED IN THE UNITED STATES OF AMERICA
NEW DIRECTIONS BOOKS ARE PRINTED ON ACID-FREE PAPER.
FIRST PUBLISHED AS A NEW DIRECTIONS PAPERBOOK (NDP1052) IN 2008

LIBRARY OF CONGRESS CATALOGING-IN-PUBLICATION DATA

CASTELLANOS MOYA, HORACIO, 1957–
[INSENSATEZ. ENGLISH]
SENSELESSNESS / HORACIO CASTELLANOS MOYA ; TRANSLATED FROM THE SPANISH BY KATHERINE SILVER.
P. CM.
ISBN 978-0-8112-1707-1 (ALK. PAPER)
I. SILVER, KATHERINE. II. TITLE.
PQ7539.2.C34I6713 2008
863'.64—DC22

2008002235

NEW DIRECTIONS BOOKS ARE PUBLISHED FOR JAMES LAUGHLIN
BY NEW DIRECTIONS PUBLISHING CORPORATION,
80 EIGHTH AVENUE, NEW YORK 10011

SENSELESSNESS

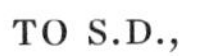

TO S.D.,

who made me promise I would never dedicate this book to her

ISMENE: My lord, the good sense one has by birth
never abides with the unfortunate,
but goes astray.

Sophocles, *Antigone*

ONE

I AM NOT COMPLETE IN THE MIND, said the sentence I highlighted with the yellow marker and even copied into my personal notebook, because this wasn't just any old sentence, much less some wisecrack, not by any means, but rather the sentence that astonished me more than any other sentence I read that first day on the job, the sentence that most dumbfounded me during my first incursion into those one thousand one hundred almost single-spaced printed pages placed on what would be my desk by my friend Erick so I could get some idea of the task that awaited me. *I am not complete in the mind,* I repeated to myself, stunned by the extent of mental perturbation experienced by this Cakchiquel man who had witnessed his family's murder, by the fact that this indigenous man was aware of the breakdown of his own psychic apparatus as a result of having watched, albeit wounded and powerless, as soldiers of his country's army scornfully and in cold blood chopped each of his four small children to pieces with machetes, then turned on his wife, the poor woman already in shock because she too had been forced to watch as the soldiers turned her small children into palpitating pieces of human flesh. Nobody can be complete in the mind after having survived such an ordeal, I said to myself, morbidly mulling it over, trying to imagine what waking up must have been like for this indigenous man, whom they had left for dead among chunks of the flesh of his wife and children and who then, many years later, had the opportunity to give his testimony so that I could read it and make stylistic corrections, a testimony that began, in fact, with the sentence *I am not complete in the mind* that so moved me because it summed up in the most concise manner possible the mental state tens of thousands of people who have suffered experiences similar to the ones recounted by this Cakchiquel man found themselves in, and also summed up the mental state of thousands of soldiers and paramilitary men who had with relish cut to pieces their so-called compatriots, though I must admit that it's not the same to be incomplete in the mind after watching your own children drawn and quartered as after drawing and quartering other peoples' children, I told myself before reaching the overwhelming conclusion that it was the entire population of this country that was not complete in the mind, which led me to an even worse conclusion, even more perturbing, and this was that only somebody completely out of his mind would be willing to move to a foreign country whose population was not complete in the mind to perform a task that consisted precisely of copyediting an extensive report of one thousand one hundred pages that documents the hundreds of massacres and proves the general perturbation. I am also not complete in the mind, I then told myself on that, my first day of work, sitting at what would be my desk for the duration, my eyes wandering aimlessly over the tall almost bare white walls of that office I would be using for the next three months—its only furnishings were the desk, the computer, the chair I was digressing in, and a crucifix behind my back, thanks to which the walls were not completely bare. I must be much less complete in the mind than all of them, I managed to think as I threw my head back without knocking myself off balance in the chair, wondering how long it would take me to get used to the presence of the crucifix, which I couldn't even consider taking down because this wasn't my office but rather the bishop's, as my friend Erick had explained to me a few hours earlier as he was leading me toward it, even though the bishop almost never used it, preferring the one in the parish church, where he also lived, so I could use this office as long as I wanted, but I wouldn't be able to get rid of the crucifix and replace it with something else, something to hang on the wall that would lighten my spirits, something that would have been as far removed from any and all religions as I was myself, even though at that moment and for the coming weeks I would find myself working there in the archbishop's palace, situated precisely behind the cathedral, another sign that *I am not complete in the mind,* I said to myself with real concern, because that was the only way to explain the fact that a depraved atheist like myself had agreed to work for the perfidious Catholic Church, the only way to explain that in spite of the hearty revulsion I felt toward the Catholic Church and all other churches, no matter how small, I found myself now precisely in the archbishop's palace facing one thousand one hundred pages of almost single-spaced text that contained the horrific stories of how the armed forces had decimated dozens of villages and their inhabitants. I am the least complete in the mind! I thought with alarm as I stood up and began to pace like a caged animal around that office whose only window facing the street was walled up so that neither the passersby nor anybody inside would succumb to temptation, I began to pace around as I would frequently do each and every one of the days I spent within those four walls, but at that moment, on the verge of going mad after realizing that I was so not complete in the mind that I had accepted and was starting a job with the church, a job that had already put me in the sights of the armed forces of this country, as if I didn't already have enough problems with the armed forces of my own country, as if the enemies in my own country weren't enough for me, I was about to stick my snout into somebody else's wasps' nest, make sure that the Catholic hands about to touch the balls of the military tiger were clean and had even gotten a *manicure*, because that was what my work was all about, cleaning up and giving a *manicure* to the Catholic hands that were piously getting ready to squeeze the tiger's balls, I thought as I fixed my gaze on the bulky stack of one thousand one hundred pages that lay on the desk, and, momentarily stopping my pacing, increasingly in a stupor, I understood that it was not going to be easy to read, organize, and copyedit those one thousand one hundred pages in the three months my friend Erick and I had agreed on: Shit! Having agreed to edit that report in just three months proved that my problem wasn't that I was not complete in the mind but that I was completely unhinged. All of a sudden I felt trapped in that office with those high bare walls, a victim of a conspiracy between the Church and the armed forces in a foreign country, a lamb being led to the slaughter thanks to a stupid and dangerous bout of enthusiasm that made me trust my friend Erick when, one month earlier—as we sipped Rioja in an old Spanish bar near police headquarters—he asked me if I would be interested in copyediting the final report of the project he was involved in, a project that consisted of recovering the memories of the hundreds of survivors of and witnesses to the massacres perpetrated in the throes of the so-called armed conflict between the army and the guerrillas, if I would be interested in earning five thousand dollars for spending three months editing about five hundred pages written by well-known journalists and academics, who were turning in a text that was almost finished, I would only have to look it over, a final proofing, it was really a great gig, five thousand dollars just to put the final touches on a project that dozens and dozens of people had participated in, beginning with the group of missionaries who had managed to record the oral testimonies of the Indians, witnesses and survivors, most of whom didn't even speak Spanish very well and who were afraid above all else of anything that had to do with the events they had been victims of, followed by those in charge of transcribing the tapes, and ending with teams of distinguished professionals, who would classify and analyze the testimonies and who would then also write up the report, my friend Erick explained to me in detail, not very emphatically, very calmly in fact, in that conspiratorial tone so typical of him, knowing that I would never refuse such an offer, not because of the enthusiasm a good Rioja might awaken in my spirit but rather because he perceived that I was so not complete in the mind that I would accept his offer and even get excited about the idea of being involved in such a project without weighing the pros and cons or negotiating, which is just what happened.

I flung open the door, terrified, as if there were no air in that closed room and I was about to pass out in a frenzied fit of paranoia; I stood in the doorway, probably with my eyes popping out of my head if the way the two secretaries turned and looked at me was any indication, determined to leave the door open while I got used to that place and my new job even though the open door would undoubtedly affect my ability to concentrate on what I was reading. I didn't care, I preferred any distraction, even if it interfered with my reading of those one thousand one hundred pages, to suffering new fits of paranoia provoked by such close quarters and my sick imagination set off by one not even very ingenuous sentence—just one among hundreds I would have to read in the coming weeks—which had sent me into a tizzy that could only paralyze me, as I confirmed now when I returned from the threshold to the chair, where I soon sat down and stared at the aforementioned sentence, *I am not complete in the mind*, and which I intended to skip over immediately in order to get to the one that followed without stopping to digress as I just had, in order to avoid the risk of getting dangerously bogged down in the job I was only just beginning, but my intention was thwarted a few seconds later by the appearance in my office of a little guy with glasses and a Mexican mustache, the guy whose office was right next to mine and whom my friend Erick had introduced me to about an hour earlier as he was leading me to my place of work, a little guy who was nothing less than the director of that entire complex of offices devoted to monitoring human rights, the second in command under the bishop, Erick explained to me as I was offering him my hand and peering at the framed and very prominently placed photographs of him standing with Pope John Paul II in one and with the president of the United States, William Clinton, in another, which immediately alerted me to the fact that I wasn't shaking hands with any old little guy but one who had given that same hand to the pope and President Clinton, an idea that almost managed to intimidate me, given the fact that the pope and the president of the United States were the two most powerful men on the planet, and the little guy who was now entering my office had had his picture taken with both dignitaries, no minor accomplishment, so I immediately stood up and asked him solicitously what I could do for him, to which the little guy responded just as kindly as possible, asking me to please excuse the interruption, he was aware that I was facing an arduous task, he said, as he pointed to the one thousand one hundred pages that lay on the desk, but wanting to take advantage of my having opened the door to enjoy what was surely my first break, he had taken the liberty of coming to invite me on a tour of the whole building so that I could meet the rest of the staff, a tour my friend Erick, always in a rush, had omitted when he led me directly from the reception area to what would be my office, stopping only at the little guy's office as I already mentioned, an invitation I immediately accepted and that carried me to each and every office in that building, which, truth be told, wasn't a building so much as a colonial structure attached to the back of the cathedral with the typical layout of an archbishop's palace: two stories of solid stone with wide corridors surrounding a square central courtyard, where we found several employees enjoying their morning break, and who, seeing me with Mynor, for this was the name of the little lay director of that institution, greeted me effusively and with some fawning, as if I were a new seminarian, while the little guy extolled my professional virtues thanks to which the report about the massacres would end up being a first-rate text, and I told myself that the good-looking girls had to be hiding somewhere, because the ones the little guy had introduced me to were not only not complete in their minds but also in their bodies, devoid of even one attractive feature, an observation I did not share with my guide and, as the days passed, I discovered to be intrinsic to that institution and not only to the extreme left, as I had always thought—that ugly women were an exclusive attribute of extreme left-wing organizations—no, now I understood that they also were intrinsic to Catholic organizations dedicated to monitoring human rights, a conclusion I reached later, as I said, and at no time did I share this with the guy who had posed for photographs with John Paul II and Bill Clinton, the little guy who took me all around, from one office to another, until finally he left me alone again in front of the one thousand one hundred pages awaiting me in my office, not before asking me if I'd like him to close the door, to which I responded that it would be better to leave it open as we were in the quietest corner of the palace and there wouldn't be any annoying interferences to distract me.

TWO

In order to celebrate my first day of work as God intended I arranged to meet my buddy Toto at noon at El Portalito, the city's most legendary cantina, fortunately located a mere two hundred yards from my office, close enough to prevent the onset of anxiety in someone who is afraid, above all else, of failing to be punctual, as is the case with me; someone who requires a drink to calm the nerves at the strangest moments, as is also the case with me, which made me consider the proximity of the archbishop's palace to El Portalito well-nigh miraculous, like a wink from the heavens that would enable me to do my work without faltering, as I explained to my buddy Toto once we were sitting down at a table in the cantina awaiting the voluminous mugs of beer, looking over the faces of the other clientele: the certainty of having a cantina so close by, right at hand, no matter what kind of office I am stuck in, lays the groundwork for a certain degree of spiritual peace, I was explaining to him at the very moment we picked up our mugs to make a toast, which Toto took advantage of to show off his peculiar sense of humor: "May you come out of this shit alive," the wiseguy pronounced in solemn tones, a joke that immediately made me suspicious of the men sitting at a nearby table, knowing as I did that all kinds of thugs hung out at that dark and squalid cantina, including informers and torturers who belonged to the so-called Presidential High Command, torturers who usually drank alone, almost never looking up from the table, their eyes bloodshot and their grimace sinister, who could be recognized by the scent of the dense, ghastly aura surrounding them. "Don't worry, take it easy," my buddy Toto told me, unsheathing his equine teeth from under his Pancho Villa mustache, then right away asking me about my impressions after my first morning of work, how had the priests treated me, I should tell him all about it, but at the precise moment my story was about to begin, a marimba thundered deafeningly from a raised dais next to the door, a marimba played by two very old men, the notes sweeping all conversation away from the tables, especially those closest to the door, like ours, and we would have had to shout in order to hear each other, which my buddy Toto then did to tell me that this music was a kind of welcome march, that he had no doubt it was dedicated to me, he shouted with a mocking grin, knowing that if there is anything I despise with particular intensity it is folk music, and especially the sad, mournful music of the marimba, an instrument only a sad and mournful people can idolize, as I have said many times. "Cut the shit, man, and tell me all about it," he said, laughing at my expense, because I didn't have much choice, given the fact that the marimba was just beginning its serenade, and I would have to shout to be heard over that sad and mournful music, something that truth be told wouldn't be difficult for me, much less now that we had ordered a second round of beers, but also I had to forget about the marimba and its irritating music in order to concentrate on telling him my impressions after my first morning of work, a story that I could begin only by describing the strange sensation I'd had when I knocked on that enormous wooden door located behind the cathedral, as if I were asking them to open the doors to catacombs I had long feared and abhorred but whose bowels I was now destined to penetrate, that strange sensation of being about to enter a forbidden and undesirable world I'd had early that morning while I waited for them to open the enormous wooden doors on that stinking filthy street already infested with street vendors and suspicious-looking characters, like the ones who also hung out at this cantina, where the marimba finally finished its first song and the waitress brought us our second round of beer. Once I'd made my way past the enormous wooden door following a porter who looked like an old sexton, I hastened to tell my buddy Toto, taking advantage of the interregnum of silence between one song and the next, I was led into a cold and intimidating waiting room, like the anteroom of a convent, where I remained alone for too many minutes while the porter went to find my friend Erick, sitting on a bench where only the prie-dieu was missing and where I could appreciate in all its dimensions the fact that I was entering a world ruled by the laws of Catholicism, which had always produced in me the greatest revulsion, which made me consider the possibility of rushing out of there at that instant, although I was immediately overwhelmed by an even stranger sensation, as if I had been there before and now had come back to relive the same experience all over again, and that it would affect my life in some definitive way, I told my buddy Toto at the very moment the marimba started playing a new song, a chilling sensation, by the way, as if I were about to live out a destiny in which my will barely counted and whose principal feature was danger.

Before continuing I should state clearly that I felt especially safe with Toto, not only because we were in his city and he knew his way around easily, but also because he looked like a landowner—the wide-brimmed hat, the military boots, and the loose-fitting jacket—thereby commanding a certain respect, who knows why, and he probably was carrying a loaded pistol on his belt—forewarned is forearmed—and Toto defined himself as a farmer and a poet, a fact I alone knew, given our close friendship, but to the rest of the cantina's clientele he would look like just a landowner, a feared species in this country due to its aggressiveness and the little consideration it showed for other peoples' lives, as might be gathered from reading the one thousand one hundred pages that lay on the desk in the archbishop's palace and about which my buddy Toto now started to interrogate me. I told him that my friend Erick had stuck it in me crooked and without lubrication, the clever asshole. Instead of the five hundred pages we had agreed on, I would have twice that amount of text to edit without Erick showing any willingness to also double my remuneration. He was confident that at that stage I wouldn't change my mind because three hundred of those pages were lists of massacres and victims' names and the other eight hundred were very well written, as I was soon to discover, and as he assured me, so my job was to only polish and touch up the final version, although of course I had carte blanche to change anything I thought necessary, without of course altering the focus—and his trust in me was such that it wasn't necessary to go into much detail, he said. And the truth was, I admitted to my buddy Toto, that the fifty pages I had read this morning were very carefully written indeed, I would even say they were impeccable, in spite of the antiseptic and slightly academic style of the psychiatrist who had written this first part of the report, a Basque by the name of Joseba, whom I didn't know and who was now out of the country, whose method consisted of proposing several theses about the effects that the specific and generalized drawing and quartering had had on the physical, mental, and emotional health of the surviving population, only to then support his theses with the testimonies of some of those survivors, carefully chosen out of hundreds and hundreds of cases that were in the archives, some of which, read this morning, had unsettled my sick imagination, I admitted to my buddy, who drank his beer a little too quickly, or rather drank while I was talking and so got ahead of me, for example the case of the village deaf-mute, I continued, I don't remember in which far-flung village up in the highlands this happened, I read it just before leaving the office, I was even mulling it over on my way as I crossed the city's main plaza, known as Parque Central, in front of the cathedral, because the poor deaf-mute had the misfortune of being interrogated by soldiers who didn't know he was deaf, the misfortune of being beaten to make him spill the names of those who had collaborated with the guerrillas, in front of the other inhabitants of the village and without saying a word the deaf-mute was beaten without saying a word after each question the sergeant who commanded the unit asked him, without anybody in the village daring to tell the sergeant that the deaf-mute couldn't answer even when they tied him to that tree in the plaza and the sergeant began to make incisions on his body with a saber to his shouts of "Speak, you Indian sonofabitch, before I really get pissed off!" but the deaf-mute just opened his bulging eyes so wide that it looked like they were going to pop out of his sockets from terror, unable to answer the sergeant, who, of course, interpreted his silence as defiance and unsheathed his machete to get him to spew out words as fast as a sports announcer and so that this herd of horrified Indians watching the scene would understand that the worst thing they could ever think of doing was to defy authority, a sergeant who was pretty stupid if we consider that he cut the deaf-mute to pieces without even realizing that his screams were not just screams of pain but also the only means for the deaf-mute to express himself. "What a stupid deaf-mute, why didn't he make signs with his hands?" my buddy Toto commented as he picked some potatoes and onions off the plate the waitress had just brought to the table, as if he had no idea that the first thing the soldiers do is tie a victim's wrists to immobilize him and as if I hadn't explained that with the first swing of the machete the god-damn hands of the deaf-mute went flying, tied and all, and that at that point nobody was about to start giving explanations with hand signals; therefore, after the deaf-mute every single other inhabitant of the village was worked over with the machete even though they knew how to talk and said they were willing to denounce the people who had collaborated with the guerrillas, but it didn't do them any good, the orgy had commenced and only a couple of them managed to survive and come and tell about it twelve years later, I said at the same moment my buddy Toto ordered his third beer while I still had half of my second one, which seemed wise, I must confess, given the fact that it would have been quite inappropriate for me to arrive drunk and disorderly at work on my first afternoon, to pound on the enormous wooden door so that they would let me in to keep reading stories like the one about the deaf-mute or to pick through the testimonies to find sentences like, *I am not complete in the mind,* just one of the many that astonished me as I went through the pages, I explained to Toto, powerful sentences spoken by Indians for whom remembering the events they told about surely meant bringing back their most painful memories, but also meant entering the therapeutic stage of confronting their past, bringing out into the open those bloody ghosts that haunted their dreams, as they themselves admitted in those testimonies, which seemed like concentrated capsules of pain and whose sentences had so much sonority, strength, and depth that I wrote down some of them in my personal notebook, I said at the same moment I took my little reporter's notepad out of the inside pocket of my tweed jacket, realizing that my buddy Toto had stopped paying attention because the cantina was filling up and some not-so-bad-looking girls were sitting at a few of the other tables. You're a poet, just listen to this beaut, I said before reading the first sentence, taking advantage of the marimba having just ended, and in my best declamatory voice, I read: *Their clothes stayed sad* . . . and then I observed my buddy, but he in turn looked back at me as if he were waiting, so I immediately read the second sentence in a more commanding tone of voice, if that were possible: *The houses they were sad because no people were inside them* . . . And then, without waiting, I read the third one: *Our houses they burned, our animals they ate, our children they killed, the women, the men, ay! ay!* . . . *Who will put back all the houses?* And I observed him again because by now he must have fathomed those verses that expressed to me all the despair of the massacres, but not to my buddy Toto, more of a landowner than a poet, as I sadly discovered, when I heard him mumble something like "Cool . . . ," to be polite, I guessed, because then he stared at me with that your-money-or-your-life look in his eyes and said that I should take it in stride, that editing one thousand one hundred pages of stories about Indians obsessed with terror and death could break even the strongest of spirits, infect me with malignant and morbid curiosity, the best thing for me to do was to distract myself, counter the effects, and, according to him, I should forget about my work as soon as I was out of the office, pointing accusingly at my notebook, I should be grateful that for security reasons they didn't allow me to take the manuscript out of the palace, because living with a text like that twenty-four hours a day could be fatal to someone as compulsive as

I was, it would ratchet up my paranoia to truly unhealthy levels, you shouldn't take that out of the priests' quarters, and he pointed again at my notebook—just think of it as any other office job, my buddy Toto said and pointed with his chin to the table next to us and behind me, where a couple of damsels were conversing with some jackass, as if this were the appropriate moment to start flirting, as if I had read him those sentences out of my notebook to convince him of the righteousness of a just cause I was committing myself to, when what I really wanted, as I told him now a little pissed off by the circumstances, was to show him the richness of the language of his so-called aboriginal compatriots, nothing more, assuming that he as a poet might have been interested in their intense figurative language and their curious syntactic constructions that reminded me of poets like the Peruvian César Vallejo, and I proceeded to read, now with more resolve and without letting myself be intimidated by the marimba that again started up, a longer fragment so that Toto could have no doubts whatsoever: *Three days I am crying, crying I am wanting to see him. There I sat down on the earth to say, there is the little cross, there is he, there is our dust and pay our respects we will, bring a candle, but when we bring the candle, the candle there's nowhere to put it . . .* And this sentence, tell me, I rebuked him, now decidedly more pissed off, if this isn't a great verse, a poetic jewel, I said before reciting it with greater intensity: *Because for me the sorrow is to not bury him my-*

self. . . . That was when I detected alarm in my buddy Toto's eyes, as if I were shooting my mouth off and some informer were taking down notes without my realizing it, which sent chills up and down my spine, and I had the reflex to look nervously at the customers sitting at the tables around us, some of whom could well have been military informers, it wouldn't even have surprised me if many of them were, given the state of affairs in that country, more reason for me to put my little notebook away in my jacket pocket and motion to the waitress to bring me my third and last beer. "To not desire, this alone I now desire," my buddy recited with a mocking smile, wiping the foam off his mustache, then said, "Quevedo."

THREE

I BLEW UP AS I HADN'T BLOWN UP for a long time, in the administrative offices of the archdiocese one afternoon soon thereafter, when the accountant told me there wasn't any money for me, that he didn't even know that he was supposed to pay me, heedless of the fact that my friend Erick had assured me that same morning that I could go by the accounting office in the afternoon to get my two-thousand-five-hundred-dollar advance, per our agreement that they would pay me half of the five thousand dollars upon commencement of the work and the other half upon termination of the same, which is why I walked from my office down the long, wide corridors to the other side of the archbishop's palace to collect the money without which it would be impossible for me to continue my work, as I explained to the accountant, so insignificant and dim-witted sitting behind his desk, and I so unwilling to believe that my friend Erick would have deceived me so blatantly. Or are you saying, sir, that my friend Erick lied to me shamelessly? I said, skewering the accountant, who kept his eyes down without responding, like an altar boy who'd been scolded, until from the back of the office a tall blond man with a Caribbean accent appeared and in a commanding voice asked what was going on, as if he hadn't already figured it out, and he stood in front of me, a situation too good to be true, here was a Crusader in the land of the Indians whose face I could rub in the Catholic bureaucracy's inefficiency, which I proceeded to do without further delay by spitting out that it was inconceivable to me that my money wasn't forthcoming, for my friend Erick had given me his word—and I pronounced "his word" with adequate emphasis—that this afternoon I could pick up my advance, and as far as I knew the word of my friend Erick was worth something in this institution, which meant that somebody wasn't doing his job and was putting the entire project at risk, because I was not willing to correct even one more line of those one thousand one hundred pages if they didn't pay me my advance right now per our agreement. No great observational ability was needed to appreciate that the blond man was busting his balls trying to control himself, incensed by my tirade, which I hadn't even finished, as he soon realized when I nailed him by saying that not only did they expect me to do twice the work for the same amount of money, which was already a pittance by any measure, but they now had the gall to flagrantly disregard the very essence of the contract, the payment of my advance, this said in a louder voice and with a touch of hysteria, I must admit, as often happens when I find out that somebody is trying to cheat me, clearly the intention of the blond man, who was now muttering between clenched teeth that I would be paid at the latest the following day, that he as the office manager guaranteed this, it was simply a matter of a short delay because he hadn't been there in the morning when Erick probably came to process the payment. Imagine how lucky I was when at that moment the little guy who had had his picture taken with Clinton and the pope appeared at the door, for if it hadn't been for his timely appearance who knows how the dispute would have ended between the blond man, who must have thought I was some kind of moron who wouldn't fight for his advance, and me, who thought that getting paid as promised had a value above and beyond everything else, as I told the little guy once he assured me—resting his supposedly calming hand on my back, a gesture that awoke in me the worst possible suspicions—that on his word as director I would be paid my two thousand five hundred dollars early in the morning of the following day, asking me moreover if I preferred to have it in U.S. dollars or in the form of a check drawn on local currency, a stupid question any way you look at it for in all my discussions with my friend Erick we had always talked about five thousand dollars, never mentioning his local currency, those putrid, old bills that wouldn't motivate anybody even minimally in their right mind, as in my case, as I said to the little guy as he escorted me, without removing his suspicious hand from my back, to the wing of the palace where we had our offices, with a slow and cadenced step, as if we were elderly priests taking our evening stroll, and he took the opportunity to suggest I not get angry at Jorge, the office manager, that the delay in my payment was not his fault, and moreover he was a good fellow, from Panama, very dedicated to the project, I would soon get to know him better. Then he asked me, wanting to change the subject and thereby help me calm down, about the quality of the text of the report I had read so far, by my third day of work, to which I responded that so far the quality was not the problem but rather the quantity, double what had been agreed upon while the time given to complete it had remained the same, as had the money, an assertion that automatically got me all riled up again at the delay in my payment, a state that persisted after I took leave of the little guy, entered my office, and closed the door behind me, then sat down in front of that hefty stack of paper without even the ghost of a chance that I could pick up where I had left off, especially because the first sentence my eyes lit upon was, *With only sticks and knives they killed those twelve men they talk about there*, followed by a short statement that struck me as lethal—it said, *They grabbed Diego Nap López and they grabbed a knife each officer giving him a stab or cutting off a small slice . . .* —because suddenly my fury grew into a paroxysm of rage, even though nobody could have imagined anything of the sort if they had seen me sitting there leaning my elbows on the desk, my gaze lost in the high bare wall, a rage focused on that despicable Panamanian who was to blame for my not getting paid my advance, who did that shit-face think he was? Didn't he realize I wasn't just another miserable Indian like he was used to dealing with? Then I stood up and began to pace around the room, by now I was utterly possessed, my imagination whipped up into a whirlwind that in a split second carried me into the office of the aforementioned, at that hour of the night when nobody remained in the archbishop's palace except that Jorge fellow there in his office, supposedly poring over his accounts but really savoring the knowledge that he had shit on me, my humanity, so focused on that thought that he didn't hear me arrive and thus couldn't react when I stabbed him in the liver, a blow that made him fall to his knees, surprise and terror in his eyes, mouth gaping, his two hands trying to staunch the flow of blood from his liver, making him even more incapable of defending himself when I stabbed him a second time under his sternum, with even greater fury this time, such was my spite, my zealous arm plunging the knife again and again into the body of that arrogant Panamanian who had refused to pay me my advance, until I suddenly found myself in the middle of my office imitating the furious movements of someone stabbing his worst enemy, of course without a knife in my hand, like a lunatic, as anyone suddenly and without warning who opened the door to my office, which I realized in dismay was unlocked, would have thought. I must admit, however, that once I sat back down in my chair, taking deep breaths in an attempt to lessen my agitation, I felt as serene as someone who has been relieved of a great burden, as if the Panamanian had in reality received his retribution and I was therefore free to leave, for there was no way I could work until those two thousand five hundred dollars were in my pocket, which is what I did, without giving any explanations to anybody, I grabbed my jacket, walked through the vestibule between the two secretaries, reached the enormous wooden door, and stepped out into the street.

For a few seconds, before I took off like a shot, I enjoyed that hour in the afternoon when the sun had not yet set, the transparent light, a warm breeze blowing through the streets at the same pace as my own steps, and that's no joke, because I was walking as fast as my legs could carry me, first on one side of the street, then on the other, crossing impetuously in the middle of the block, not so much to prevent somebody from following me, how deluded could I be on such a crowded street, but rather to avoid the ambush I always feared, the one in which two pseudo-muggers—really army intelligence operatives—would corner me and stab me to steal something I didn't have on me so the priests would finally get the message, I was a foreigner whose murder in the course of a street crime would have no repercussions. At all costs avoid the always-feared ambush: I had this goal in mind every time I went out, obsessed, electrified, just like that afternoon they didn't pay me my advance and I threaded my way down Octava Avenida, a street stinking of piss and garbage that led from the archbishop's palace to the central market, a dunghill behind the cathedral I walked through with long strides, constantly scanning the field—behind, in front, to the sides—as if by descrying the murderer's face I could guarantee my escape, down a stretch of sidewalk crowded with people and street vendors, another stretch on the asphalt the old buses clambered down noisily, overusing their horns, not slowing my pace until I reached Novena Calle and turned up toward Pasaje Aycinena, my improvised destination, because before going to my apartment I wanted to have a few drinks, I wanted some distraction, and the place I picked was a shabby bar-café named Las Mil Puertas, which, despite the name, had only two doors, not a thousand, territory of recycled communists but above all frequented by young men and women with artistic inclinations, bohemians, rebels perhaps, in any case an ambience as different from the archbishop's palace as could be, tender slabs of young flesh to lift my spirits, I told myself once I was inside and sitting at the corner table, ready to order a soda to catch my breath, because in that joint they served flat water, which I prefer, from the tap, a dangerous circumstance I'd learned about during my previous visits, when I had also sat at the corner table where the walls were marked up with those horrible verses written by mediocre left-wing poets, hawkers of hope, verses written without humility, in big prison-style lettering, but even so, a table that was preferable to those outside, along the Pasaje Aycinena, a deserted walkway that led from Novena Calle to the entrance of Parque Central. So I ordered a whisky with soda and set about clearing my head of all mental associations related to my work at the palace, just as my buddy Toto had advised me to do, taking note instead of every single one of the girls in this bar-café, the good-looking ones, of course, who were few in number but enough to distract me, one of them in particular, a thin girl with lively eyes, oriental eyebrows, and a laugh that was flirtatious for being somewhat timid, whose features sparked my imagination so powerfully that I could picture, within seconds, as I rubbed the palms of my hands against my eyes, that girl's face as she was being possessed, penetrated, shaken by my rhythmic assault, and I could also see her expression of total abandon at the moment of orgasm and almost hear her plaintive moans, like a satisfied cat, an exercise in fantasy that managed to stabilize my mood and even generated a weak current through my groin, nothing to worry about, even less so now that they had brought me my whisky and soda and after relishing the delightful tickle of that first sip, I finally recovered my equilibrium and relaxed, capable now of observing the flow of my thoughts while remaining separate from them, not identifying with them, as if they were somebody else's mental movie I was watching with a certain amount of indifference, a mood propitious for achieving spiritual peace but which I couldn't hold on to for as long as I wanted due to the arrival of a group of persons whom I identified at first glance as belonging to the office I had recently fled and which at that moment I didn't want to remember anything about, a truly impertinent interruption, for their appearance not only shook me abruptly out of my mood but also forced me to ask myself what the hell I was doing with my life, committing myself to such a project and having to dash madly around a foreign city, which is what I had just done by taking the longest route so as to throw off any possible pursuers, according to my thinking, as if in the end I wasn't going to find my way to this joint where any wretch could nab me if he wanted to. But I wasn't going to allow that group of so-called defenders of human rights to ruin my whisky for me, I told myself as I took another sip, and I proceeded to take my notebook out of the inner pocket of my jacket intent on calmly relishing those sentences that seemed so astonishing from a literary point of view, an observation I would never again share with insensitive poets like my buddy Toto, sentences I could, with luck, later use in some kind of literary collage, but which surprised me above all for their use of repetition and of adverbs, such as this one that said, *What I think is that I think* .... Wow. And this one, *So much suffering we have suffered so much with them* ...: its musicality perplexed me when I first read it, its poetic quality too high not to suspect that it came from some great poet rather than from a very old indigenous woman who with this verse had brought to an end her wrenching testimony, which wasn't the point at the moment. Both sentences should have been written on the walls of this bar-café instead of those horrible verses by leftist poetasters, I thought as I put away my notebook, asked the waitress for the check, and took one last look at the girl with oriental eyebrows whose face had fired up my imagination. Upon leaving I walked right by the table where my colleagues were sitting, though I refrained from greeting them, still irritated by their inopportune appearance, and they didn't greet me either though there passed between us one or another look of recognition.

FOUR

BINGO: I FINALLY FOUND A good-looking girl. Allow me to clarify: she was no Demi Moore, but she had all her parts in all the right places, was well-proportioned, had fine features and a healthy expression, without that resentment so typical of those ugly doyens of messianic causes who thronged the archbishop's palace, a girl born in Toledo, Spain, who had spent most of her life in Madrid, in the Salamanca neighborhood, which is no slum, and whose father was a well-known military physician, an admirer of Generalísimo Franco, whom he served under, she told me, but not when we first started talking, obviously nobody introduces themselves like that, much less so in the courtyard of the archbishop's palace, full of so many so-called guardians of human rights, where she was reading and soaking up a little morning sunshine, sitting on the rim of the stone fountain. An apparition! I said to myself, Lord in Heaven! as I walked down the corridor toward the kitchen to get a cup of coffee, but there and then changed my direction toward that apparition, next to which I sat down, introduced myself without any preambles, and immediately asked her where had she been hiding all week, how was it possible that I hadn't seen her, hadn't even known of her existence until that very moment. She told me her name was Pilar, otherwise known as Pilarica, a graduate in psychology from the Complutense University of Madrid, for the past five months working under the supervision of my friend Erick in the archbishop's palace but also in indigenous communities in the province of Alta Verapaz, where she had been the previous week, that's why we hadn't met. A few hours later, at noon, we walked together through the large wooden door on our way to a vegetarian restaurant located in front of the bandstand in Parque Central, conversing in a relaxed fashion, the first time I had left the archbishop's palace with someone else and without the devil nipping at my heels, a pleasure no matter how you looked at it, walking along and chatting calmly with an attractive girl, a foreigner and apparently intelligent, who moreover worked most of the time just a few feet from my office and with whom I could easily establish a closer relationship, too good to be true, as I soon discovered, for we hadn't even reached the vegetarian restaurant when I began to detect certain expressions that made me suspect that my delightful companion might be a fanatic of that nonsense called political correctness, which put me slightly on my guard and thereafter made me think that the very fact that we were about to enter a vegetarian restaurant already constituted one alarming symptom, for only a mind accustomed to absurd abstractions and fashionable activism could prefer that insipid food to a good cut of tender juicy meat, which is why so far I hadn't dared ask her why she had chosen that restaurant for our first meal together, hoping she would allege some digestive ailment resulting from her sojourn in inhospitable regions, but no, just as I feared, once we were seated in that environment infused with a certain sect-like air, which I immediately perceived, Pilar began her diatribe against meat, which was not only repulsive to her but also very unhealthy, enumerating the various harmful, even deadly, effects of ingesting meat, with a lexicon and an emphasis appropriate for the daughter of a military physician and Franco supporter turned savior of indigenous peoples, which is what she did on her trips to the countryside, she met with indigenous communities, victims of the atrocities committed by the armed forces, to help them overcome the trauma they were suffering as a result of not being able to go through the traditional mourning rites, she explained to me, for the worst thing was the absence of cadavers for sinister reasons, which prevented people from carrying out any mourning rituals, as a result of which they suffered all sorts of disorders, something I was already familiar with, as I told her, that's what the report's all about, so familiar that I proceeded to take my notebook out of the pocket of my corduroy blazer to read her a few remarkable sentences related to the subject she had just brought up, and I placed it on the table, open, next to my plate of soup: *My children say: Mama, my poor Papa where might he be, maybe the sun passes over his bones, maybe the rain and the air, where might he be? As if my poor Papa he was an animal. This is sorrow . . .* , I read between spoonfuls, and then I looked for a sentence that had electrified me that very morning: *The pigs they are eating him, they are picking over his bones . . .* , I enunciated as I reached for my glass of myrtle juice, because they didn't serve beer at that restaurant, a sip of something to soothe my throat so I could continue reading the sentence, *I want to see at least his bones,* but at that moment I perceived that Pilar was not enjoying my sentences, the astonished expression on her face indicated as much, as did her stillness, so I decided to close my notebook but not before reading, only to myself, the last of the sentences that I would have liked to share with her, which said, *While the cadavers they were burning, everyone clapped and they began to eat . . .*

Luck would have it that the following evening after work I went out with Pilar to have a few beers—thank God she wasn't abstemious—to a bar called La Bodeguita de Enfrente, a rather odd name, for across the street from this bar, per the name, there was nothing besides a barbershop, and in spite of the diminutive ending in the name it was a large bodega whose walls were plastered with hundreds of posters with revolutionary slogans and at night they had live music, either the keening imitators of the so-called New Cuban Song, or danceable tunes in the style of the Gipsy Kings, but when Pilar and I arrived it was still early, only a few tables were occupied, and we found the best possible conditions for conversation under the congenial influence of the beer, I even revealed to her certain aspects of my life, a vice I am not addicted to, like the fact that a month before I had been forced to leave my country because I had written an article that stated that El Salvador was the first Latin American country to have an African president, a statement that was characterized as "racist" and that won me the enmity of half the country, especially those with power and my employers, despite my subsequent clarification that I was not referring to the fact, anyway verifiable, that the president looked like a black African, for the color of his skin didn't matter at all, but rather to his dictatorial attitude and his refusal to hear the opinions of those whose opinions differed from his, I explained to Pilar, therefore a month ago I was forced to immigrate to this country, my neighboring country, and accept my friend Erick's offer to edit the report she already knew about and was also working on. "How did you meet Erick?" she asked, as if I were confessing rather than carrying on a lighthearted conversation under the congenial influence of the beer, and after making vague reference to us having coincided in Mexico during my exile and his graduate studies there, I went on the offensive, now she was the one who had to loosen her tongue, come on, and I asked her with full impunity if her boyfriend also worked at the offices of the archbishop, my only intention being to jar her ever so slightly, never dreaming that I had touched her gangrened wound, as I was soon to find out, for what at first was simply a suddenly altered facial expression quickly became an outburst of tears, an inferno, abject discomfort, a human specimen crying because—I was certain—of so-called love, who would proceed to find in me a captive audience she could spill her guts to—still sucking in her snot—about her tragedy: the guy was named Humberto, he had also been working for the archdiocese when they met—*how did you know?*—but three weeks ago he left for the Basque Country to study for his Master's in Political Science, none of which justified her tears, I told her rather sharply; nobody in their right mind would cry because their lover had gone away to study, unless he had gone with somebody else and was sleeping with that person, I said, irritated, because the most irritating thing is a crying woman and her nose started dripping even more freely and she demanded I tell her who had told me about it, as if one needed a gossipmonger's loose tongue to discover what I had figured out using common sense, I explained, already decidedly uncomfortable, with the waiter eavesdropping from behind the bar—*we don't want another beer, you gimp!* I would have loved to shout at him, but at that moment Pilar began wailing uncontrollably about how he had betrayed her since the very beginning of their relationship, but she had only realized it when Itzel, her victorious rival and, needless to say, colleague had also traveled to the Basque Country, just one week after Humberto, for no reason and without any explanation, she said still sniffling loudly, to which I responded that the reason resided in Humberto's crotch, speaking as an expert on couple relationships, and then I offered her my best homily: it's a sign of an intelligent person to be grateful when they manage, without the slightest effort, to rid themselves of a treasonous and slimy partner, in view of the fact that this immediately and without further ado renders them free to initiate a new relationship that will allow them to open themselves up in a way they never could with the traitor who didn't deserve them anyway. And I smiled at her, so she would fully understand my words. But Pilarica returned to her old ways, sobbing in a frankly grotesque manner, with no respect for me, who just wanted to drink a few beers and explore the possibility of seducing a girl who appeared to be good-looking and intelligent, what a crass mistake, mucus doesn't exactly enhance beauty nor tears intelligence, so I gestured to the gimp to bring a couple more beers, getting ready to stand up in deference to my bladder, but at that moment and in a quick broadside she muttered that what hurt her most was that she had lovingly loaned her darling Humberto one thousand dollars and he had turned right around and used it to pay for an airplane ticket for that very same Itzel. *Damn!* I blurted out at the gimp, who nervously placed the beers on the table. Did you hear that? This girl pays for her boyfriend's lover's trip, how many of us have got a girlfriend like that . . . ! The victim of her own stupidity suddenly stopped crying, sat rigidly up in her chair, as if she had just woken up from a dream, dumbfounded, perhaps tempted to become indignant, it seemed, and in response I raised my mug of beer and said, Cheers, not thinking precisely of her but rather of Humberto, a clever fellow from the looks of it and with a great future ahead of him, not to mention Itzel, whose total lack of scruples had fired up my imagination, which led me to ask Pilar what kind of creature was that girl who had taken her, Pilar's, money to run off with her, Pilar's, boyfriend, such a perfect scheme that it could only have been conjured up by a woman, but my serious and indignant companion didn't utter a word. For the moment I found myself in an uncomfortable situation, for there is nothing more repulsive to me than a woman who cries as a result of her own stupidity and who in addition asks for my commiseration, but at the same time nothing so stimulates my fantasies as the possibility of fornicating with a good-looking girl recently abandoned because of her own stupidity whom I could delightfully take advantage of during the act of love, so I didn't know whether to tell Pilar that we should call an end to our tearful date and proceed to pay for the beers we had drunk, or, on the contrary, activate my strategies of seduction so as to move things forward. My razor-sharp intuition told me that she was undergoing a similar conflict, on the one hand very upset that I had made fun of her stupidity, especially in front of the gimp, but on the other needing company and perhaps not wanting to go home right away only to sink into the murky mire of mortification. Fortunately, at that instant, two enthusiastic guys who worked at the archbishop's palace appeared at our table, very good friends of Pilar's, apparently, whom I knew only by sight, and without further ado they sat down, ordered beers, and managed to unravel the knot that had tangled up our date, which I interpreted as a sign from the heavens that I should persevere with Pilar because a good romp in the hay, if it were possible, would calm my nerves and gratify my senses after a week of being shut in a room reading about cadavers and torture.

When, after eleven o'clock, we got into a taxi that would take us to Pilar's apartment, I already had indigestion from the two hours I had spent swallowing one song after another of the much-lauded New Cuban Song movement sung by a primate with long curly locks who made Pilar a member of the chorus par excellence, for the Toledan screamed her head off as if by doing so she could recuperate the thousand dollars and her lost boyfriend, while I gulped down my beers, already a bit irritated, though I was very careful not to show it, until finally the primate with long curly locks ended his set, and Pilar looked at her watch with a start and said that she had to work the next day, the look on her face like that of a schoolteacher scolding her young charges, then stood up and asked the waiter to bring us the bill, which favorably impressed me considering the quantity of beer she had inbibed and the unsteadiness of her gaze, for I had assumed I was going to have to remove her feet first from that Bodeguita de Enfrente, which didn't happen, but instead both of us got into the taxi that would supposedly take us first to her apartment, where she would get out, and then to mine, where I would get out, another event that didn't happen as expected because when we arrived at her apartment it was suggested that I should take advantage of the opportunity to see it and have one last beer, with her consent, of course, it could not have been otherwise. I forgot to say that Pilar was a typical Spanish girl: thin, with a big ass, small bust, thick eyebrows, a turned-up nose, a nasal and rapid-fire voice; in her plaid skirt she climbed the stairs to her second-floor apartment, followed by my greedy eyes on her swaying ass I was tempted to grab, but we weren't on such intimate terms yet, despite our flirtations at La Bodeguita de Enfrente and one or another inadvertent brush against each other, so I deferred my attack until we were in the kitchen and after she had taken a couple of beers out of the refrigerator, God's will be done, my mouth on her mouth, which was not open enough for my liking, my hands caressing her neck, her back, then tightly squeezing her lovely buttocks, which would soon have to become meat to sink my teeth into, which I longed to do, while I led her, without releasing our mouths nor removing my hand from her buttocks, toward the sofa in the living room on which we fell horizontally, and I proceeded, directed by logic, to suck on her little tits and then, with one audacious move my palm was on her pubis and my middle finger slid into her dampness, something so natural that her subsequent reaction left me utterly crushed, because suddenly she turned into a teenage virgin who'd been warned that the wolf comes disguised as a cock, my God, and she pushed me aside and sat up and said, "I can't," with two thousand years of guilt drying out her cunt, repeating "I can't" to convince even herself, her face twisted in a grimace of pain, because things with Humberto were so fresh for her that she was incapable of making love with another man, that I should forgive her, that I should understand her, that it had nothing to do with me, that until she had gotten over what had happened with Humberto she wouldn't be capable of being with anybody else, she insisted, even though she liked me and she felt good with me, she just couldn't. And then all the listlessness in the world fell upon my shoulders—I had gone to the wrong theater, which was showing a boring old movie I could follow with my eyes closed because I'd seen it so many times—a listlessness so overwhelming and paralyzing that I didn't even have the wherewithal to stand up and get myself a taxi, which I should have done, but instead crawled into an armchair facing her, clutching my beer, and resigned myself to watching Pilarica act out her melodrama about that clever young man and that perfidious colleague, a whole litany about one's self-esteem blown to bits, the tears and snot *de rigueur*, until I had no choice but to return to the sofa where she was sobbing, comfort her, allow her to cry on my shoulder while I sniffed at her hair, because she used a shampoo I wasn't familiar with, one that had a strong scent, to tell the truth, almost unpleasant, and while I comforted her I could feel how soft the skin on her arms was and slowly I again began making maneuvers, with some hope, to see if I could breach her defenses with a second assault. I must admit this kiss lasted longer, I could even make her open her mouth the way I liked, my hand also lifted her plaid skirt and caressed her thighs, with largesse, delighting in her pubic hairs, even though they were a little thick for my taste, but the moment I approached her cunt and began to encircle it, she pulled my hand away, whispered "no" but didn't push me away, as if I were going to spend the whole night kissing her and getting hornier and hornier, so I decided to make a radical move and I went down on her to eat her out, and once and for all stick my middle finger up her ass, sonofabitch, my balls were about to burst, but suddenly she got up, a modest young lady at the far end of the couch, better to leave things as they are, she said, stern but without any reproach. I'm leaving, I said. Then she softened up, but not in the way I wanted her to, instead she said, "Don't go, I don't want to stay here alone," she needed company, the girl she shared the apartment with was away, another Spanish girl who worked at the offices of the archbishop and was traveling through indigenous regions, and I could sleep in her bed instead of risking going out so late at night, she said, standing up and taking my hand so that I would follow her, to which I acquiesced because if at first you don't succeed, try, try again, and in her bed, all the better, for I still wasn't intending to give up, by the way, that's why I barely paused in Fátima's room, that was her roommate's name, but rather accompanied Pilar to her quarters, where the bed looked wide enough for us to frolic to our heart's content, the desk was too small and the titles of the books on her shelves rather horrifying, as I told her when she was on her way toward the bathroom, I presumed to get ready for bed, and while I waited for Pilar to emerge in her short transparent baby doll, as sexy as could be, I set about riffling through her belongings, in the beating of a bird's wings, but the fact is I was waiting for the Toledan to give me a pleasant surprise, which is why when I saw her come out in one of those Franco-style pajamas worn in the convents of bygone eras so that the novices couldn't get even their own hands onto their own private parts, my astonishment was absolute, I could only exclaim, And *that?!* never having seen such a garment, a garment she had surely inherited from her mother, or had been given to her by a strict mother superior, pajamas that really looked like a spacesuit, the only thing missing was the astronaut's helmet, I thought, still amazed, so much so that I asked her if under that spacesuit she wasn't also wearing a chastity belt, for I had never seen one in my life and she should let me see it, I begged her, but instead of answering me she crawled under the covers, said she was exhausted, and asked me to please turn off the light.

FIVE

WHEN I WOKE UP THAT MORNING I could never have imagined the dirty trick that had been played on me. For a few minutes I remained serenely between the sheets in my apartment in the Engels Building, dozing, receiving in my cupped hands the warmth of my testicles, happy in the knowledge that it was Friday, listening to the cries of the street vendors that rose to my fifth-floor apartment very early in the morning, because my apartment with high ceilings and large windows was located on the corner of Sexta Avenida and Once Calle, in the very heart of the city, as I realized once again that morning upon opening the curtains and contemplating the light on the rooftops and between the buildings, which fortunately were few within my immediate visual perimeters; a furnished apartment with housekeeping services—laundry and fresh sheets and towels like in a hotel—I moved into almost immediately upon my arrival in this city, and whose rent of four hundred dollars a month didn't seem too excessive given its privileged location, which allowed me to walk the six blocks that separated it from the archbishop's palace and to have my favorite bars right on hand, and given its very good security situation thanks to a guard being on duty twenty-four hours a day. Once I was dressed and groomed and had eaten my yogurt and cereal—health always comes first—I double-locked the door, walked down the hallway to the elevator, pressed the button to the first floor, got out in the lobby, where I said good morning to the receptionist and the doorman, then went straight out onto the street, keeping my eyes on the passersby, walking down Once Calle on my way to Octava Avenida toward Café León, where I could drink the best coffee in the city and peacefully read the newspapers, as I did from Monday to Friday, before making my way to the office, I sat down at the bar and asked for a café latte and a couple of churros and grabbed whatever newspaper was available, which that Friday morning turned out to be a rag called *Siglo XX*, which I read without finding anything of much interest until I got to Polo Rosas's column, where to my surprise I saw myself mentioned in a most ignominious way, that hack whom I'd met only a few times in my life when I lived in Mexico stated in the aforementioned column that I had told him that so-and-so had told me that another so-and-so had been opposed to Polo Rosas being awarded a prize for his novel ten years before, which of course left me flabbergasted not only because of the false nature of the information but also because the entire rigmarole had been drummed up to prove that I was some kind of snitch, which would have been nothing worse that insignificant gossip if I didn't find myself at that moment carrying out a delicate task whereby the genocide perpetuated by this country's army against the unarmed indigenous population was being documented and exposed, making me almost choke on my coffee, and I didn't feel like even tasting my churros when I realized that this was a clear message from the Presidential High Command letting me know in no uncertain terms that they knew I was in that city, involved in what I was involved in, which wasn't really a surprise to me, considering the high quality of the military intelligence services, the surprising aspect being that they would employ some hack with a reputation as a leftist rebel to communicate this message to me and, I then understood, to the church as well, in order to make them distrust me and my work by having Polo Rosas insinuate that I was a snitch, which of course perturbed me excessively, I almost started screaming and waving my arms around at the bar in the Café León because such libel was a vicious assault on my amour propre and at the same time unleashed my paranoia to such a degree that I no longer wanted more coffee or my churros, but instead I paid and left for the palace, choking on my rage, certain that my friend Erick and the little guy named Mynor had already read the aforementioned column and might know something more about it. But neither of them was in his office when I was so eager to discuss with somebody this dirty trick Polo Rosas had played on me, not only to extract the knife from my wounded amour propre, as mortifying as that was, but also to analyze the significance of this maneuver and discuss what means should be taken to counteract it, to which end I shut myself up in my office and called my buddy Toto, after all a farmer and a poet and therefore acquainted with the local literary fauna, and suggested that we go get a couple of beers around midday, at eleven, to be more precise, at the usual place, as I had a deadly hangover, I lied, without ever mentioning Polo Rosas's dirty trick, so as not to give the military, which was taping every telephone call that came in and went out of the palace, the pleasure of knowing how deeply their knife had pierced me. I must admit that from eight-thirty in the morning, the moment I passed in fury and poisoned spirits through the enormous wooden door, until ten forty-five, when I passed through it again on my way to El Portalito, I couldn't concentrate on my perusal of the one thousand one hundred page report, I spent the whole time planning one or another way of responding to the calumnious column written by that hack, whom I'd only seen twice in my life and about whom I remember nothing but his bald spot, and the impertinence and resentment he brandished about once he'd downed his first drink, nothing else, just his bald spot with a few graying tufts around the edges that, due to a highly inexplicable and circumstantial association of ideas, made me repeat again and again like one possessed a sentence written on the piece of paper on my desk, which I immediately copied into my notebook and which said: *There in Izote the brains they were thrown about, smashed with logs they spilled them,* which I repeated with increasing fury until I could see those magnificent logs making pieces of gray hair tufts anointed with brains fly through the air, nor could I make even a modicum of progress because neither my friend Erick nor the little guy with the Mexican mustache would be coming to the palace that morning, according to one of the secretaries, for they were attending an important meeting at the bishop's parish church, as far as I could figure out, which further inflamed my paranoia and made me afraid that libelous rag would be the first item on the agenda. I was right to assume that my buddy Toto had not read the aforementioned column, as he confessed to me when I found him installed at the corner table, having arrived ahead of me because he really was suffering from a terrible hangover. "I don't read that shit," he said without attributing any importance to the matter and after criticizing me for wasting my time and even worrying about what some slum lord had written, who everybody knew was the eyes and ears of G-2, the so-called military intelligence, as I had correctly inferred, because Polo Rosas was not *sensu stricto* a novelist but rather the owner of many rental units in various neighborhoods in the city, whose legal representative and rent collector was a lawyer who also worked for the military, my buddy said while still half asleep in the cantina, thank God with no marimba playing and where we were the only customers other than a couple sitting lazily at the bar, which explained why the novels the old guy had published were exclusively about deserters and snitches from the ranks of the guerrillas, and even worse, it was known that said person on two occasions had joined a left-wing guerrilla group and come out of it unharmed while most of his comrades had been murdered, my buddy Toto said, without assigning too much importance to it, as if he were talking about some clerk who filched paper from the copy machine and not a slanderer who, in the light of these new revelations, had acquired a sinister aspect, I asserted with my paranoia firing up yet again after the poet and farmer stated, "Cut the shit, if the sonsabitches want to send you a message, the very least they'll do is give you a pounding," which was precisely what I most feared, a vicious attack with a knife in the middle of the street, and then he said that if they wanted to give me a pounding they didn't need to go through some old bald guy with prostate disease who probably just wanted to use his newspaper column to irritate me, which is precisely what he had achieved. I didn't have a chance to respond to Toto's analysis because at precisely that moment we saw walk toward our table Chucky, the Killer Doll, a short stocky guy who looked just like a bulldog with blue eyes, whose subordinates, including my buddy Toto, affectionately dubbed with the name of that movie character, Chucky, the Killer Doll, as much for his appearance as for the fact that in his youth he was known as playing a leading role in all kinds of dangerous adventures in which he had risked his own life and taken the lives of others, even though he was now the respectable director of an NGO dedicated to promoting the municipal power company, where my buddy Toto worked in public relations, lives like those of the four soldiers who had tried to capture him seventeen years before when he was a daring left-wing urban guerrilla commando, when he and his main comrade-in-arms were taken by surprise by soldiers who believed they'd gotten the upper hand once they had tied their wrists together and loaded them into the back of their jeep, not expecting Chucky and his comrade to strike back so fiercely that the four soldiers in the jeep were killed while Chucky lost only his baby and ring fingers on his right hand, an adventure I had heard about many times from the mouth of my buddy Toto as well as from the hero himself, who now with a few pints under his belt brandished said stumps, which I felt when we had shaken hands, after he greeted us with the typical, "What's happening, you faggots!?" before he sat down and started clapping loudly as if he owned the place to get the waitress to rush over and take his order. And then Chucky blurted out the morning's good news: that a few hours ago the main opposition presidential candidate had miraculously escaped an attempt on his life in Zone 9. "You're kidding," my buddy Toto exclaimed, who in spite of being the public relations person for the NGO had not read the column against me nor had he heard about the assault, while his boss knew about both events, as I later discovered, when he told me that Polo Rosas was an envious old bastard nobody would ever trust enough to hire for a delicate task like the one I was performing, thanks to which Chucky was immediately transformed from a likable assassin into an intelligent and clever guy, a conclusion further re-enforced when he recounted with a flourish of colorful details an incident that had occurred fifteen years before when urban commandos under his leadership had likewise attacked the presidential candidate of the main opposition party, at that time the Christian Democrats, the difference being that in that instance the whole thing had been a mistake, Chucky said unable to hold back his laughter: all-terrain vehicles with tinted windows had been seen driving out of a fortified mansion surrounded by dozens of bodyguards, making it look like the center of operations of the right-wing death squads, and given the sense of urgency during that period and without doing any research, he had decided to launch an assault—the immediate reprisal for the death squads' attack on a university press—that consisted of machine gunning and throwing grenades at a car driving out of the compound, after which the commandos retreated without any difficulty, until they were surprised to hear on the radio that they had just attacked the home of Vinicio Cerezo, the Christian Democratic candidate and subsequently president of the republic, who fortunately had come out of it unharmed, he hadn't been driving in the machine-gunned car, and he was holding the right-wing death squads responsible, Chucky said with a flirtatious chuckle, because at that moment the waitress, whom he constantly called "my love," had brought him a plate of toast smeared with beans, and that handsome guy, that blue-eyed bulldog, might even manage to score with her, but for that he needed something more than daring and bravery, and he continued recounting anecdotes that distracted me enough to draw me out of the perturbed state the newspaper column written by that treacherous bald and big-eared hack had put me in.

The afternoon of that same day I met briefly with the bishop for the first time, in my very own office, which was in fact his office, the head honcho came with the little guy with the big Mexican mustache to meet me and find out how the report was coming along, a tall robust man with a bearing that commanded respect, like the godfathers of *La Cosa Nostra* as well as the high ecclesiastical dignitaries of the Vatican, I understood at that moment that this bishop, of Italian descent, could very well play Marlon Brando's role in *The*

Godfather, perhaps with even more conviction, which gave me a positive impression, considering that my image of priests after years in a Salesian school was that they were a bunch of faggots, crows in cassocks, their eyes full of perversion, which didn't correspond in the least to this stately silent man who asked few questions, preferring to stare inquisitorially at how my hands were moving, something that had never happened to me, to feel exposed through my hand movements—*damn!*—as if I were suddenly confessing all my sins through my hand movements. I explained to him that the report could be divided into four volumes, the first two containing the bulk of the aftermath of the massacres of villagers, the third containing the historical context, and the fourth consisting of a list of the massacres and their victims, and that in this way the one thousand one hundred pages would be more manageable for the reader, I specified, and although I, at that point, had only read carefully through half of the second volume, I could assure him that we were dealing with a text of the highest quality, I said, as if the purple-robed man had not long before reviewed everything that had landed on my desk—and at that moment I was especially discomfited by the attention he was paying to how my hands were moving, so I crossed my arms over my chest—a text that was precise in its analysis and with some very moving testimonies, fascinating, especially that richly expressive language, on a par with the best literature, I proclaimed, and I was about to pull out my notebook to regale the bishop's ears and those of the little guy named Mynor with the sonorous sentences that had so excited me, but just as I was about to do so I realized that they might think that without authorization I was removing in my notebook information we had clearly agreed I would not take out of that office, so instead I returned to the pages of the report that were on my desk and read the first underlined sentence I found that said: *Even at times I don't know how resentment arises or who to take it out on at times . . .* The bishop stared at me, an indecipherable look in his eyes behind his glasses with tinted lenses and tortoise-shell frames, a look that made me afraid he might see me as a deluded literati seeking poetry where there were only brutal denunciations of crimes against humanity carried out by the army against the indigenous communities of his country, that he would think that I was a simple stylist who wasn't paying any attention to the content of the report, so I abstained from reading any further sentences and instead began to talk about the structure and the table of contents, the psychosocial focus and the classification of the mental afflictions of the victims, but without the godfather shifting the object of his indecipherable gaze or saying a word, all of which made me extremely nervous, understandably so, for nobody likes to face an inquisitorial priest listening as if expecting a shameful confession, that's how I felt, and I definitely would have revealed to him my frustration that the only good-looking chick I had met in the archbishop's palace had refused to lend me her splendid ass if the little guy named Mynor had not mentioned that in a few moments they both had to welcome an important delegation from an international organization, and so, as if with the pealing of a bell, I was rescued from succumbing to the inevitable confession and also prevented me from talking to the little guy about the implications of the dirty trick that had been done to me and published that morning in that rag *Siglo XX*.

SIX

THAT SUNDAY I STAYED IN BED until ten in the morning, for moments dozing off, fantasizing about Pilar, but not managing to concentrate long enough to jack off properly because suddenly the name of Itzel would seep into my mind, a name without a face that awoke my prurience through strange sinuous mental pathways, and soon thereafter so did the name Fátima, the Toledan's roommate, whom I would meet that afternoon when the three of us would go to eat ceviche and have a few beers, as Pilar and I had agreed on Friday, when I saw her at the end of the day in the courtyard of the archbishop's palace and mentioned to her my brief meeting with the bishop—still impressed by the fact that the head honcho would focus in that particular way on my hand movements—as well as one testimony that seemed like the plot of a novel I had once read and that on that Sunday morning came back to me along with an urge to take it on and release all restraints on my imagination, for in fact no such novel existed, only the desire to write it, to turn the tragedy on its head, to turn myself into the suffering ghost of the civil registrar in a town called Totonicapán, an idiot whose foolish behavior led to them cutting off with a machete each and every one of his fingers, sliced off he saw his phalanges fall one by one as the soldiers kept him pinned to the ground after they had beaten him so hard they had broken who knows how many bones to teach him not to underestimate them and that dedication to one's work had a limit and that this limit was the authority of the lieutenant, who now brandished the machete, letting fall one decisive blow that split the head of the civil registrar of Totonicapán longitudinally, as if it had been a coconut and they were at the beach and not in the battered living room of the civil registrar's house, splattered with the blood and brains of the aforementioned, who had refused again and again the lieutenant's request to turn over the village's register of the dead, who knows why he behaved so foolishly, for the lieutenant urgently needed a list of the villagers who had died in the previous ten years so he could bring them back to life so they could vote for the party of General Ríos Montt, the criminal who had taken power through a coup d'être and now needed to legitimize himself through the votes of the living as well as the dead, so as to dispel any doubts, something the civil registrar of Totonicapán never understood, not even when the contingent of soldiers broke into his house and he knew his fate was sealed, not even when he felt the sharp blows that sliced off his phalanges did he admit that such a register was in his hands, even as they were being amputated, although the register did exist and he had hidden it under some firewood in his backyard, according to my version, because the testimony didn't give many details, he had preferred to die rather than turn the register over to the lieutenant from the local garrison, for this is precisely what the novel would be about, the reasons why the civil registrar of Totonicapán had preferred to be tortured and murdered rather than hand over the death register to his executioners, a novel that would begin at the precise instant the lieutenant, with one stroke of the machete, split open the head of the civil registrar as if it had been a coconut from which he would remove the delicious white pulpy flesh, not the bloody palpitating brains, which may also seem appetizing to some palates, I must admit without any bias, the instant that blow fell the restless soul of the civil registrar would start to tell his story, always with the fingerless palms of his hands pressing together the two halves of his head to keep his brains in place, for I am not a total stranger to magical realism. The story would begin with the explanation that the soul of the registrar would remain in purgatory until somebody could enter him into the death register, which was very difficult to do given the fact that he alone knew where he had hidden it, which is why the story would center around the efforts of the civil registrar's soul in purgatory to communicate to his friends so they could write him into the death register without the military finding out, and through this would be revealed the history and the significance of that register, which had been in the hands of his family for generations, a son and grandson of civil registrars dedicated to their profession, that is, a story of suspense and adventure that I should have begun cobbling together that Sunday morning while I was still lying under the sheets with my thoughts playing some kind of disorganized ping-pong game, if at the time I had been a novelist, needless to say, and not just a copy-editor of barbarous cruelties who dreamed of being what he was not.

I should stop this foolishness, I told myself, throwing back the sheet and jumping energetically out of bed, on my way to the bathroom to take a shower, determined to control once and for all my fantasies, committed to my goal of not jacking off so as not to squander my mental energy, of not wallowing in any of the testimonies that I would never turn into a novel, because nobody in his right mind would be interested in writing or publishing or reading yet another novel about murdered indigenous peoples, and it was the last straw that on the weekend I would carry on in the same vein as I did when I was in the archbishop's palace as if they were paying me to poison my days off, I scolded myself, while I waited for the water coming out of the shower head to warm up, hoping that Fátima would be as good-looking as Pilar but without those emotional cobwebs left behind by embittered loves, as I'd already gone a month and a half without a fuck, ever since I arrived in this city I had been condemned to chastity as if they were getting me ready to don the habit, I thought once I was under the stream of warm and comforting water, soaping my groin and my balls, pulling on my penis but with my mind set on scrutinizing my wardrobe, for I was determined to look handsome and sporty so the girls would sigh, to which end I chose a polo shirt, salmon-colored, faded blue-denim pants, and brown leather loafers. Putting on my shoes, there I was, when five shots rang out in the street below, five unexpected and piercing shots that I began counting after the first rang out, which I guessed had come from a nine-millimeter-caliber gun, but five, not six as the doorman claimed later, with the inanity so typical of a fool who doesn't pay attention and just gets scared, because he had to dash into the building to take refuge while I jumped up and looked out my fifth-floor window, trying to catch a glimpse of something, smelling the scent of gunpowder that rose from the street, eager to try to discover the source of such an unexpected event, for after a month and a half in this downtown apartment these were the first gunshots I had heard, my curiosity spurring me on so strongly that one minute later I was in the lobby of the building arguing with the foolish doorman, who insisted that there had been six shots and that it was a car chase, like in the movies when the car doing the chasing shoots at the car being chased, so there were neither victims nor traces of the shootout in the street, he told me already back at the front door, where I could ascertain that apparent normality reigned among the street vendors settled under their plastic shades on the sidewalk. I walked over to the guy who sold pirated CDs, encrusted into the corner of Sexta and Once, about ten steps from the entrance to the building, to ask him what he had seen. "Nothing, I threw myself on the ground," said the short fat mestizo man without looking me in the eyes, as if I were a policeman who had come to investigate the incident, when all I wanted to know was how many shots he had heard, five like I—who had paid attention—claimed, or six like the doorman—who lost his concentration when he rushed inside—claimed, to which the vendor responded that he also hadn't paid attention, there could have been five or six, he mumbled, the height of imprecision; so I insisted, explaining to him that there could only have been five shots because after the first one I began counting out loud, an old habit I had acquired during the war in my own country, saying, two, three, four, five, and I remained with the word six in my mouth because there was no sixth shot, and moreover I could be certain that they'd come from a nine-millimeter gun, that my ear wasn't just any old ear, and if we looked for the bullet casings down the street we would be able to prove the truth of my assertion that the shots had come from a nine-millimeter gun, I told the vendor, who pretended not to know what I was talking about, and, pretending to be busy, he began to dust off the pirated CDs with a flannel rag. I crossed the street, there was very little traffic that day, and in front of McDonald's I bought two Sunday newspapers—but not that rag that I will never again mention in whose pages I had been maligned—hoping to eat my breakfast while perusing the articles and also so I could ask the newspaper vendor about the shooting that had just occurred, but he turned out to be a worse case than the guy selling pirated CDs, so from there I decided to continue walking down Sexta Avenida under the splendid morning sunshine, not allowing the bad smells and the garbage in the street to soil my soul, content to think that no passerby or street vendor could intuit my thoughts, walking in the direction of the restaurant of the Hotel del Centro, where the buffet of local cuisine would be my Sunday breakfast throughout my stay in that city, at a time of day when the only disturbance came from a marimba that at regular intervals attacked the clientele, but such disturbances were a plague common to all restaurants.

Life is marvelous, I exclaimed to myself, about three hours later, marveling at the sight of the girl with Pilar, that very same Fátima about whom I knew so little until that moment and who was about to become the object not only of my attentions but also those of half a dozen indolent beasts drinking beer in the Modelo Cevichería, a kind of food kiosk with a few plastic chairs squeezed onto one side of the small plaza in front of the Conservatory, half a dozen beasts among whom I ought to include myself a bit shamefacedly and who were stupefied and drooling as they stared at the two girls crossing the street in front of the Conservatory and approaching down the plaza's sidewalk toward the cevichería, I, possessed of the knowledge that they were Pilar and Fátima, while the others were simply aroused by the prospect of such gorgeous girls, apparently foreigners, coming to perfume that cevichería, where the main attraction was the Sunday soccer match between Mexico and Argentina on the television. Approach, dear ladies, your appearance serves the singular purpose of delighting these ridiculous potbellied men in their stupid shorts, I would have liked to say to them as a greeting, if those same potbellied man hadn't had on their faces a certain threatening look and if their ears weren't just a little too close to my words, attentive as they were to that pair of sweet things, who both gave me kisses on both of my cheeks, lighting up my day and darkening the lives of the potbellied men, who soon began to secrete a poisonous envy because the girls ignored them and sat down—so deliciously—very nearly one on each of my legs, an envy mitigated only by the soccer match between Mexico and Argentina though they could no longer concentrate on the game with the same intensity, every once in a while looking libidinously at the girls as they ordered their fish ceviches and beers in a pleasant exchange with the waiter. The first thing I knew about Fátima was that I wanted to lick her all over due to the appetizingly creamy texture and light rosy hue of her skin and her perfect curves pressed into a pair of red-denim jeans and an organdy blouse under which could be descried her seductive belly button as well as a little path of fuzz my eyes began to follow, descending, while she talked about her recent trip to a village in the high-lands, where years ago half the population had been slaughtered—initiated by the army but with an enthusi-asm that left no room for doubt—by the other half, their fellow citizens, one of the 422 massacres contained in the one thousand one hundred pages that awaited me on the bishop's desk the following day, when I would continue my task of copyediting and correcting and about which I refused to think, wanting only to descend the peach-fuzz path that would carry me from Fátima's belly button to her fleshy cave, where I wanted to take refuge from those potbellied spies, from the television sportscasters with diarrhea of the mouth, and from the sudden and unexpected memory of the hundreds of In-dians I had strolled among a few hours earlier in Parque Central while I peacefully digested my breakfast and passed the time, enjoying the brilliant morning among these hundreds of Indians decked out in their Sunday dress of so many festive colors, among the most salient being that joyous cheerful red, as if red had nothing to do with blood and sorrow but was rather the emblem of happiness for these hundreds of domestic servants enjoying their day off in the large square surrounded by the cathedral, the presidential palace, and the old commercial arcades, a splendid and telling promenade because as I wandered around under that brilliant sky I realized that not one of those women with slanted eyes and toasted brown skin awoke my sexual appetite or my prurient interests, thanks to which I continued walking lightly and mincingly, my fantasies remaining dormant, attentive rather to the patterns on the textiles and the cut of those ethnic costumes whose colorful skirts prevented the exposure of even the tiniest patch of skin, the opposite of what was transpiring with Fátima's flirtatious belly button, which was winking at me, luckily without the potbellied men realizing it, for they were fascinated by the battle of the Titans, as the sportscaster defined it with a howl that caught the attention of even the two girls, for whom soccer was, of course, boring, but who couldn't detach themselves wholly from the reigning emotions, to the extent that Fátima even asked me who I was rooting for, Mexico or Argentina, and as my third eye had already detected some antipathy toward the Aztecs oozing out of said potbellied men, I immediately told her that all of Central America was rooting for Argentina against their giant criminal neighbor, spoken with enough emphasis to guarantee me safe conduct out of there flanked by two such girls as these.

SEVEN

SUCH A NOVELTY IT WAS WHEN I finally met the Spaniard who had planned and executed half of the one thousand one hundred pages I so intrepidly continued to correct, the Basque named Joseba so loved and admired by everybody in the archbishop's palace, according to what my friend Erick and the little guy named Mynor told me when they introduced him to me, a Basque and by profession a psychiatrist, for that was the only way to comprehend how he would have gotten involved with such enthusiasm and attention to detail in that morass of suffering that anybody in his right mind would have run away from without the slightest hesitation, as I gave him to understand once we were alone in my office going over the corrections I'd made to his text, which was already so clean and clear, only a psychiatrist from the Basque countries could have immersed himself for months in studying with such dedication the testimonies of hundreds of victims traumatized by the orgy of blood and dust, which they had come out of alive only by chance, I told Joseba with outright admiration, and then I read out loud and as if in passing a few sentences I had copied down in my notebook and that were highlighted on the pages I was leafing through on my desk, sentences like, *Then he got frightened and went crazy completely* or *That is my brother, he's gone crazy from all the fear he has had; his wife died from fear also,* or, *It's not just hearsay because I saw how his murder was,* or this that impressed me so much, *Because I don't want for them to kill the people in front of me,* sentences that proved the extent of mental perturbation of the survivors and the danger that such a state of mind posed for people working with them, which wasn't Joseba's case, who to all appearances exuded not only health but also a striking spirit, was tall and strong, with an upright bearing, just as I imagined those knights-errant who came to conquer the indigenous peoples of this land, an amusing idea I couldn't help but mention, as an aside, when he asked me my impressions of his work, and I repeated that he had done a superb job, impeccable, after which the history of this country would never be the same, not a chance, and taking advantage of an interstice I said to him: what a paradox, that someone so fitting the archetype of the Spanish conquistador should dedicate himself with such devotion to recovering the indigenous peoples' massacred memories, no offense intended, I clarified, because Joseba shifted uneasily in his chair in front of my desk, so modest, discomfited by my adulation, rubbing his stubbly chin. I am very impressed by the combination of objectivity and courageous humanitarianism in your text, I exclaimed with an almost feminine flair, as if I had been Fátima, which wasn't all that gratuitous since the previous afternoon she had not stopped praising Joseba as we walked toward her house in Zone 2, and so much praise could only infuse my fantasy with the most tenacious suspicions, for although this Joseba fellow was married, I would not have been surprised if he had shed the pellucid armor of a loyal knight-errant in order to enjoy the favors of said compatriot and admirer, thus it was not so very unusual that while discussing his work behind the closed doors of my office I began to fantasize that Fátima had gone up to the door and locked it, then started getting it on with him, Dulcinea herself, passionately making out with the much-admired knight as she unbuttoned his fly and extracted his lance, which she then caressed in her hands and then in her mouth and soon thereafter frenetically inserted into herself, mounting the knight who would in his alarm lose all sense of decorum, still sitting in that chair with that tasty panting morsel pounding herself against him, his gaze lost in the tall bare walls, trying not to notice the crucifix, alone and contemplative from its great height, worried that Mynor or Erick would knock on the door and discover him in such a trance or that I would suddenly appear and not only catch him with his hands in the pot but berate him for using my office to fornicate with the girl of my dreams, a betrayal capable of unleashing in me a rage that began at that very moment to inflame me against not so much the Spaniard, who was meticulously describing the methodology he used for his psychosocial research, but my own fantasies, so foolishly bent on imagining Fátima galloping on top of Joseba, instead of imagining me galloping on top of her, which would have been preferable from any and all points of view. It was the sudden irruption—after a quick perfunctory knock—into my office, which really was his office, of the Sicilian, the head capo, that shook me out of my rapture and brought me back to the scene where we were greeting each other, and he asked Joseba to accompany him to Mynor's office, where the three of them would meet to hatch a conspiracy I was fortunately not included in, I told myself, thank God, for I already had quite enough with the one thousand one hundred pages without also getting involved in Vatican intrigues, though I cannot fail to admit that merely seeing that I was unexpectedly excluded from the circle of power, in which my friend Erick would undoubtedly be included, made me feel a certain amount of resentment, as if the priest had been suspicious of me ever since he watched how my hands moved, as if my work weren't important enough and my opinions about the report didn't count. "Hey, let's have lunch together," the hidalgo said, with a wink, before leaving with the bishop, conscious perhaps of the marginalization I had been subjected to, probably afraid of the possibility that I would express my resentment by marking up the text, something that of course never even crossed my mind, as I let him know a few hours later when we were in the Imery Restaurant, located on the other side of Parque Central, a rather dark place where the menu du jour was consumed by dozens of office workers, low-level politicians, one or another academic from the institutes of higher learning in the vicinity, as well as the staff of the archbishop's palace, among whom Joseba and I could be counted, sitting at a corner table, where I readied myself to hear delicious secrets straight from the mouth of the gallant knight about the palace intrigues he had participated in that morning and about all the other intrigues related to the report that my friend Erick had failed to reveal to me, but as the minutes went by and we turned our attention to the main course, I ascertained that the Basque psychiatrist responded with monosyllables and evasions to my enthusiastic questions, as if prudence and caution were essential components of his nature, I thought at first, as if the heads of that religious institution had taken vows of silence that required absolute discretion even toward a trusted employee like myself, or, I then thought, as if they had discussed at that morning's meeting to which I had not been invited how much they could trust me and their conclusions were reflected in the Spaniard's polite negatives in response to my questioning, then I frankly grew concerned, on the verge of descending along a paranoid spiral that would in no way help my digestion and that I instantly tried to avoid by shifting the gist of the conversation, insisting instead on digging into my table companion's private life, knowing for a fact that prudence and caution were fundamental components of his character and that he would never reveal anything about his political activities in Bilbao, would never mention anything about his past and present as an ETA sympathizer, which could be smelled from a mile away, and talked only in generalities about how well one drank and ate in that city full of always crowded and welcoming bars, of shipyards, and of the shells of abandoned factories along the length of the river. But to my surprise, perhaps once he saw that the table next to ours had remained empty, Joseba suddenly changed the vague and nonchalant tone of his discourse and began to tell me, with a conspiratorial air copied from my friend Erick, that the missing text of the second volume of said report was extremely sensitive, a detailed analysis of how the army's intelligence services operated, he said, almost in a whisper, uncertain if any of the other diners could hear us, that at the meeting I had not been invited to that morning they had talked precisely about that analysis of the military intelligence services and had agreed that this text would not be incorporated into the report until the very last minute when it was about to be sent to the printers, not only for reasons of security but also because my friend Erick needed the maximum amount of time to finalize it, considering the fact that he was the lead investigator into the activities of the military intelligence organizations as well as the coordinator of all the other parts of the report, Joseba made clear, as if I were not already fully aware of the responsibilities of the person who had hired me, and the only new thing I now learned from his conspiratorial whisperings was that those people really didn't trust me, and that neither my friend Erick nor the little guy with the Mexican mustache had had the courage to tell me so but instead had sent the gallant Spanish knight to me to break the news that I probably wouldn't see or correct the report's chapter about the military intelligence services because of a problem with the deadline. I was just about to react to such a dirty trick with the stentorian indignation it deserved without caring at that moment about the waitress who had arrived with our next course, when that cunning fox, perhaps intuiting the imminent arrival of a squall, asked me as if in passing if I knew what The Archive was, with as much candor as if he were mentioning a child's bookshelf or the drawer he keeps his puzzles in, a question that couldn't fail to cause me the greatest astonishment, so much so that it took me a few seconds to react, stunned by my interlocutor's imprudence, for nobody talked about The Archive in public, much less in a restaurant just a few blocks from the presidential palace in whose chambers The Archive had its headquarters, a restaurant where more than a few officials and specialists from that sinister office undoubtedly ate on a daily basis, an office Joseba had named so light-heartedly and that I never would have named in the same way, or in any way, because suddenly I was in the grips of a panic attack, stoked by a furtive glance from the waitress before she pushed the swinging doors that led into the kitchen, a glance that in other circumstances I would have interpreted as natural feminine interest in the good looks of the hidalgo caballero, but which at that moment brought on instead a panic attack that paralyzed me, bathed me in sweat, surely made my blood pressure shoot sky high, because The Archive was in fact the office of military intelligence where the political crimes mentioned in the report had been planned and ordered, the report that lay on my desk and was written by none other than the Spanish gentleman who sat there with his mouth hanging open, at that moment waiting with such composure for me to begin to blab on about the unmentionable office, something that was not about to happen, because when I managed to overcome my stupefaction, when finally I was able to get over my panic attack, it was thanks to another shot of adrenaline produced by the fact that the waitress had brought desert and coffee when we had just begun to eat our entrees, a common practice in restaurants serving office workers always waiting for a free table at the lunch hour, I would have thought at any other time, but not then, when such haste seemed like proof that the woman was an informer for the military, a woman who already had us in her sights and wanted only to confirm the subject of our conversation before denouncing us, at which point and without rhyme or reason I launched into a feverish long-winded speech this Joseba person didn't expect: What I admire most about Spain is the struggle of the Basque people, I told him, stumbling over my words, and within that struggle I am most fascinated by the ETA tactic of executing its victims with one bullet to the back of the neck, their audacity to take them by surprise, to take advantage of them being unarmed civilians and having their backs turned to dispatch them without them even noticing, I told him with an intensity I achieve at moments, the idea of executing your victim under such circumstances can only be the brilliant result of a daring strategy that does not allow for the most minimal chance of defeat, the idea of training Basque youth in the practice of and admiration for such perfect crimes wherein the defenseless victim lacks any capacity to react seems to me capable of inspiring in those youth only the most distilled form of nationalism, I added almost breathlessly, while the waitress placed both cups on the table with the expression on her face of someone who is not hearing what she is definitely hearing, and Joseba was astonished, as if he didn't know whether he was facing an insolent provocation or a delirious rant, when the only reason for my tongue's incoherencies was to sidestep the subject that struck me with terror and to overcome my panic attack, which ceded only under the spell of my harangue, which, given my interlocutor's discomfort and without my knowing why, led me to immediately speak about the virtues of Spanish democratic tolerance, the constitutional monarchy's broad-mindedness, which allowed it to unflinchingly open the pages of its leading magazine to an indigenous woman who had survived the massacres thanks to which Joseba and I were earning a few dollars—he more than I, I assumed with good reason, given the dimensions and erudition of his work—as well as the Spanish royal family's humanitarianism and that of all the other European monarchs, who not only welcomed the aforementioned indigenous woman with their most exalted protocols but also had their pictures taken with her and allowed those pictures to be published in nothing less than the magazine *Hola!*; a short round chubby indigenous woman surrounded by kings, princes, marquises, and counts, just like in a fairy tale, I said in the same stumbling tone of voice; an indigenous woman whom none of the white, and so-called respectable, families in this country where we were now drinking coffee would have welcomed through the kitchen door unless she were delivering tortillas, that same indigenous woman who had won the most prestigious international prizes was the only citizen of this country to have appeared in *Hola!* surrounded by European royalty, a truly impressive occurrence, I told Joseba, my voice almost out of control, to have appeared in *Hola!* was the highest honor a famous person could aspire to and something this country's arrogant white masters would never forgive the chubby lady for because there was not then and never would be any chance of them ever appearing in those prestigious pages, though to tell the truth what had most impressed me about my most recent perusal of *Hola!* had been the feminine attributes of that Norwegian woman Prince Felipe was going out with, my goodness gracious, I could practically taste that Nordic flesh, I told Joseba, sucking on my teeth with relish, now a bit more relaxed, there wasn't one princess among all of those who appeared in the pages of *Hola!* capable of outshining that female Viking Don Felipe took his pleasure with, I managed to say with my last breath at the same time as Joseba stood up with an indecipherable expression on his face, indicating that we should go to the cashier to pay for our food, while the prying waitress pushed on the swinging doors and entered the kitchen.

EIGHT

LYING IN THE BED, THE RECENTLY possessed body snoring beside me, I was taken by surprise by an idea, an idea that suddenly blinded me, the idea that hell is the mind not the flesh, I became aware of this at that moment, the idea that hell resided in my agitated mind—distraught—and not in the sweating flesh, for in no other way could I explain the fact that there I was in my bed in my apartment in the Engels Building, unable to enjoy the splendor of Fátima's milky-white skin, a skin that in other circumstances would have delighted all my senses, but whose proximity had now plunged me into a state of such dire agitation that I would have given anything for her not to be there, for nothing to have happened between us, for everything to have been just one more of my fantasies. But no, I told myself as I tossed and turned in bed without being able to fall asleep, with anguish gnawing away at the mouth of my stomach, no, that body I had so strongly desired had only made me understand the vulnerability of pleasure, its fragile and crumbling nature, I reproached myself, unable to find a comfortable position that would allow me to fall asleep or even relax, my gaze fixed on the windows whose curtains I had not closed completely and through which midnight and its suspicious sounds entered; that body so desired by everybody had suddenly lost its charm when just one hour before she had asked me point blank if I'd rather she suck it or masturbate me, a question that didn't make any sense considering the fact that we had been kissing and touching each other passionately for only three minutes—a few seconds more, a few seconds less—on the couch in my apartment, and what should have followed, after she already had my member in her hand and I had my middle finger inside her pussy, was to get totally undressed and lick each other all over until we consummated the act of love, instead of her posing that indecent and inappropriate question as to whether I preferred a blow job or a hand job, as if that whole preamble of confessions, caresses, and kisses that had begun in that beer joint Tustepito as evening was falling had been only a ruse to bring on the moment when she could ask me what I preferred, a hand job or a blow job, something I'd expect from a shrewd prostitute showing her price list to a horny client rather than this Spanish beauty whom, according to me, I had seduced with my charm. Who knows what expression she saw on my face, but she immediately explained in no uncertain terms that she didn't plan on fucking me—*damn it!*—that she had a boyfriend whom she loved very much and who would arrive in the country the next morning, a boyfriend she would never be unfaithful to, even though at that very moment she held my member in her hand and was offering to let me choose if she would jerk me off or suck it, she repeated, instead of getting naked and giving herself to me as logic would dictate. I told her to suck it, because it wouldn't have been a good idea to remain aroused and with my balls bursting, such a strain causes pain and makes walking difficult, even though the magical moment had already passed, that instant when the magic of possession rises resplendent had gone to the dogs the moment she asked that indecent question, more typical of a professional than a girl who's been seduced, I thought as I contemplated her with my member in her mouth, sucking, with agitated and slightly arrhythmic movements, which made me worried I would sustain an injury, perhaps the scratch of a canine, so I suggested she calm down, take it more gently, resting my hands on her head, not concentrating too much on the pleasure she was supposedly giving me but rather attempting to figure out what difference it would make as she was reaffirming her fidelity to her boyfriend, who would arrive the following morning and whom I had just found out about, if she had given me a blow job or been penetrated, a difference that was frankly difficult for me to discern, much more so when she tried to talk without taking my member out of her mouth, saying something like "ca-cu-ca-ci," and looking at me worriedly and without diminishing the flurry of her movements she mumbled over and over again in a guttural way "ca-cu-ca-ci," with such concern in her eyes, until I told her that I couldn't understand what she was saying, that she should take my member out of her mouth before talking, which she did immediately and then she clearly repeated what before I had heard only as "ca-cu-ca-ci," which in fact was the question, "Are you happy?" I would be lying if I didn't admit that this situation surpassed all my expectations, for Fátima posed such a question with the vocal intonations of a young whore, just starting out, anxious and eager to please her client, insecure about her ability to employ techniques she had so recently learned. "Ca-cu-ca-ci," I repeated to myself in disbelief while she stuck my member back in her mouth and carried on with her dazzling performance without me being able to fully enjoy such suckling efforts, given the alienation that awkward and unprecedented situation—so much for adjectives—had immersed me in, but without, thank God, my member failing me, in which case I don't know what would have happened. And soon my absence would become unpleasant, my state of withdrawal would succumb to an overwhelming attack on the senses, when she, thoroughly excited by my member in her mouth, finished taking off the garments she was still wearing, including a pair of military boots and thick socks that seemed to me vulgar and unattractive garments to wear under a summer skirt, a fashion shared by most of her European colleagues and that I had assumed was nothing more than a youthful whim without any further consequences, but that at that moment acquired a sinister dimension when an odor issued forth from those military boots that tore my nasal passages to pieces and made me feel the strongest possible revulsion, an odor that undoubtedly permeated her feet, perhaps beautiful and appetizing from afar, but which I didn't even dare to look at because I had thrown my head back against the couch, my eyes closed, my face wearing the enthralled expression of a man overwhelmed by pleasure, when the truth was that the most diverse images and thoughts were racing through my mind, thoughts and images I clung to tenaciously so as not to succumb to the overpowering assault on my nostrils emanating from the odor of Fátima's feet. No other circumstance explained how I could have been unaware of the precise instant she stopped blowing me and in one abrupt movement climbed on top of me, only my total state of distraction made it possible for Fátima to begin to gallop on top of me with my member inside her without my realizing it, because by the time I was able to react she was already being penetrated by my member and the only thing I could do was pull her toward me so I could bury my face in her neck so as to filter out as much as possible the unbearable stench, which by then had permeated the small living room of my apartment and would probably be difficult to remove from the rug where she was digging in her feet to better ride me. Lucky me that my irrigation systems didn't let me down, for flaccidity at that moment would have been the last straw, and while she was well on her way to a state of frenzy and even as I was attempting to use all possible means to press my nostrils against her skin, my mind was bouncing around like a ping-pong ball from her previous absolute refusal to fuck me to her little shouts now presaging orgasm, from the question about my preference for a blow job or a hand job to the unintelligible "ca-cu-ca-ci," from the baneful military boots to the boyfriend who would arrive the following day; a ping-pong ball bouncing with increasing intensity as Fátima approached her orgasm and shouted, "my love," "my dearest love," as if I were the boyfriend she awaited so anxiously, whereas the only circumstance of any urgency for me was to get her off me so I could quickly go and get the air-freshener out of my bathroom. That nature is capricious I understood once she, satiated and breathless, noticed that I was still aroused, an erection that didn't correspond even remotely to my state of mind and in the face of which Fátima decided to stick my member back in her mouth after saying, "Hey, man, aren't you ever going to come?" at which point I reproached myself for not having the courage to push her aside, I hated that obsessive need I had to make a good impression and my fear of hurting someone that prevented me from asking her to stop, from telling her that it had all been a big mistake, that she should relax and go to the bathroom to take a shower while I made the bed, though I really would have preferred to call a taxi that would take her home right away. But I didn't say anything, instead I let her keep at it until I suddenly understood that coming would be the healthiest thing to do, that I should cut the crap, concentrate on the suction she was applying and forget everything else if only to prevent my balls from cramping up and in the hope of recouping some of my losses from that nonsensical night, but it was already too late and after a while she took my wilting member out of her mouth and said she was tired, that we should go to the bedroom and get under the sheets, which I agreed to, since the situation had already spun totally out of control. And she walked in front of me, giving little flirtatious jumps without me sighing for any of her body's undeniable attributes, all obscured by the disagreeable idea that the stench of her feet would permeate my bed and oblige me to ask for a change of sheets ahead of time, my bed that would no longer be what it had been, even less so when she, already lying down, immediately began telling me about the boyfriend she was expecting the following day, a major in the Uruguayan army stationed in this country as a member of the U.N. forces overseeing the implementation of the peace accords signed by the government and the guerrillas, a tender, affectionate guy who at that very moment was probably packing his bags in a New York hotel room, his heart set on the girl who the following day would meet him at the airport and who now lay beside me, naked under the sheets; a military man she affectionately called Jay Cee, for that was what he liked to be called, Fátima explained to me, even though his name was Juan Carlos Medina, Major Juan Carlos Medina, to be more exact, he preferred that she and his friends call him thus, Jay Cee, two initials that I repeated to myself, without speaking them, on the verge of panic, while Fátima revealed to me her decision to go live with Jay Cee in a few days, that the plans had already been made and she would move her belongings from Pilarica's place to the large and modern apartment Jay Cee had rented in the city's exclusive Zone 14, a move that—as she herself admitted as she was curling up in bed—betrayed some of her principles, especially those related to the poverty and suffering of the indigenous peoples she worked with, and that would also be somewhat inconvenient given the scarcity of public transportation in that wealthy neighborhood. But her relationship with Jay Cee was above and beyond all that, she said, lying face down, the sheet half-covering her back, he was an incomparable guy, mature, twelve years older than her, very understanding, so much so that they shared everything that happened in their lives, including "parallel encounters" as she called them, referring to their infidelities, because they had spent several periods of time apart, when he worked at the U.N. headquarters in New York and she traveled into the highlands, she mumbled sleepily between yawns, though until then, throughout their entire seven-month relationship, only Jay Cee had confessed with total frankness to one insignificant "parallel encounter," which Fátima had understood and forgiven, though she had not had anything to confess. You're not going to tell him about us, I whispered cautiously, for my fear had by now become too much, knowing that the girl falling asleep beside me was the fucking property of a soldier, shit, that I was on the verge of sliding away headlong on a sled of terror and was searching blindly for the tiniest branch to grab onto, but Fátima barely even turned her head, the palms of her hands joined under her cheek like a pillow, she told me that of course she would tell him, that was their agreement, to always tell each other the truth, to always trust each other totally, and that she hated pretending and lying more than anything else. I didn't want to turn her over to see for myself, nor argue in favor of silence, but instead I figured this was a joke, her way of making fun of me, even though her tone of voice didn't leave any room for doubt, sooner rather than later she would reveal our relationship to the soldier, and he would react like any cuckolded man, with the same blind rage, but even worse given the fact that we were talking about a soldier accustomed to resolving his problems through the use of arms, and since he wouldn't shoot her, he would shoot me, most probably, or both of us, I told myself as I descended into an expanding maelstrom of paranoia. I was then going to ask Fátima not to be unreasonable, that she shouldn't let her mouth run away with her, to tell the truth sometimes is foolishness itself, even suicidal, as was the case here, when it was obvious the soldier had tangled her up in his web of full confessions for his own sinister reasons, that she would drag my dignity through the mud between her feet and in the most irresponsible way she would put my life in danger; I was about to demand that Fátima not be so naïve, that she use some common sense, when she started snoring shamelessly, curled up in a little ball, serene in her deep sleep, untouched by my anguish, leaving me in a suffocating state of internal agitation, right on the verge of collapse and the only thing I could think to do was turn off the light and lie down in the bed as stealthily as possible, as if we could thus go unnoticed, as if in this way I could erase once and for all that equivocal night, nothing but torture for me, a night in which the pleasures of the flesh had been but a thin pretext for plunging me into the inferno of the mind, as I already said, because in that semidarkness penetrated by suspicious sounds I understood that I had become the target of that Jay Cee, that it would be effortless for him to kill me and blame my death on the local military thanks to the fact that I was the copyeditor of the one thousand one hundred pages that documented the genocide they had perpetrated against their so-called compatriots, or what was even worse, I thought, tossing and turning in bed, the bloodhounds of army intelligence, already informed about my "parallel encounter" with Jay Cee's girl, would liquidate me and turn my death into a crime of passion, a magnificent three-pronged strike that would allow their act to simultaneously resonate among the priests of the archdiocese, their Spanish colleagues, and the U.N. forces, all of whom were determined in one way or another to cause the army problems. There's no question at all that I was in the grips of the worst of all terrors, as if death were breathing alongside me, as if the snores of sleeping beauty were the blast of the trumpet announcing the arrival of the black heralds, what a thought, for fear distorts everything and I was experiencing tachycardia, sweating, probably with my blood pressure sky high, absolutely certain that now I was really in danger. I'd had enough: I stood up, my anxiety gushing out, and went to the living room where I could pace like a prisoner in the tower, that's how I felt, with the death sentence snoring in my bed and the prospect of a long and sinister night, unless I could gulp down a triple whisky, a substance I didn't possess, or take a strong dose of Lexotan, the sedative I was supposed to take 1.5 milligrams of in the morning and a similar dose at night, as the doctor had prescribed several months before, when I suffered from such episodes after the publication of my article about the first African president of my country, which forced me into exile, a sedative I religiously kept at arm's length, not taking the prescribed dosage, afraid as I am of addictions and knowing that with my compulsive personality I would have taken it until I'd overdosed. I swallowed two pills of 1.5 milligrams each, and I sat down to read the long information sheet that came with the medicine, a glass of water in my hand, determined to distract myself, to no longer think about the consequences of my relationship with Fátima, to reduce my anxiety so that I could then go to bed and try to sleep, which—according to the text I was reading—would happen in no sooner than thirty minutes, the time it took the pill to take effect, so that while still in the throes of dejection all I could do was collapse onto the couch, the scene of the catastrophe, and pick up my notebook from the coffee table and leaf through it and focus my attention on other voices, other rooms, but as soon as I opened it I found the last sentence I had written down before leaving the archbishop's palace, a sentence that perturbed my spirit even further, the sentence, *If I die, I know not who will bury me,* spoken by an old Quiche man whom the army had left in the direst possible situation after killing his children, grandchildren, nieces and nephews, and all his other family members, in such an extremely dire situation that this survivor's last lament in his testimony was, *If I die, I know not who will bury me,* the poor old man, a matter I immediately questioned myself about, a question that landed on my snout like a black butterfly because I didn't have anybody to bury me in case either this Jay Cee or the specialists of the so-called military intelligence decided to eliminate me, nobody to take care of my mortal remains if something happened to me, I thought with sadness, not even the few remaining family members in my own country, and no one I knew in this foreign country would take care of my bones, I bemoaned in a state of self-pity, perhaps only my buddy Toto had enough affection for me to take up a collection for the funds needed to give me a dignified burial, so my cadaver wouldn't remain in the morgue until it was sold as so much offal to some medical school, I told myself with tears in my eyes, on the verge of despair, because I felt utterly forsaken, not suffering as much as the old indigenous man whose statement had gotten me into such a state of mind, I must admit, but almost as alone and abandoned as him, even though a girl was sleeping in my bed, the intensely desired girl who had possessed me without my getting any pleasure out of it at all and whose imprudence now threatened to push me to my death. I returned to the bedroom to lie down under the sheets, to breathe rhythmically, trying to concentrate on the air coming into and going out of my nostrils, ignoring the stench of Fátima's feet, for I had other worries now, determined as I was to make that ping-pong ball bounce less and less, until I finally fell asleep.

NINE

WHAT A SURPRISE I HAD THAT morning when I found out that the beautiful and mysterious woman I saw infrequently in the corridors of the archbishop's palace was the same girl whose testimony I was proofing, testimony that had upset me so much that I couldn't complete the task in one sitting and had decided to go out to the palace courtyard to get some fresh air and a bit of morning sunshine; such a surprise it was when Pilarica, whom I found sitting on the edge of the fountain looking over her notes and also enjoying the sunshine and fresh air, told me that the woman who at that very moment was walking along the half-lit palace corridor was the same girl whose testimony I was telling her about with great trembling, for this girl recounted the infamies she had suffered seventeen years earlier in the hands of the military when she was arrested during the brutal repression of student protests right downtown in the capital city, a girl who at the time had been sixteen years old and was taken to the dungeons of the police station, where she underwent the worst degradations, including being daily and systematically raped by her torturers, a testimony given so strikingly and with so many details that it had impelled me to leave the bishop's office where I was working to find some fresh air and less disturbing emotions. "Teresa is a lovely girl, do you want me to introduce you?" Pilar asked me under the comforting morning sunshine and with her best smile, which I could reply to only with a look of consternation—not more than five minutes earlier I had been editing the text of Teresa's testimony about the most abominable rapes she had been subjected to by the soldiers who tortured her—the last thing I felt like doing was looking her in the face, which I had visualized as covered with bandages and full of bruises and bloody cuts, the face of a girl savagely beaten by her torturers in order to get her to admit that she was a member of the guerrillas and to snitch on her comrades, though the truth was that the torturers knew that the girl wasn't a member of the guerrillas, that her only sin was being the daughter of a labor lawyer who defended the trade unionists and who would be assassinated a few months later, according to what I read in the aforementioned testimony, a girl they had lowered into Hell itself for a whole week with beatings and rapes that tore apart her vagina and anus, a sweet young thing up on whom a half-dozen soldiers led by a lieutenant named Octavio Pérez Mena unleashed the worst possible cruelty, according to her testimony, an officer this woman had recognized from archive photos and who had made himself out to be the good guy, the one she should confess to so that those half-dozen beasts under his command would stop raping her and beating her, according to her testimony, who at that point was Lieutenant Octavio Pérez Mena, though with the passage of time he would become the chief of military intelligence, for torture is the measure of intelligence in the military, and who now, seventeen years later, was a respectable general strutting smugly around this same city where the woman walking down the corridors of the archbishop's palace would recognize him and feel the same terror she felt then. "Thank you. I'd rather you introduce me to her another day," I answered the Toledan, having had the thought that the imagination is a bitch in heat, without understanding exactly why precisely at that moment hammering in my head was the thought that the imagination is a bitch in heat, when nothing in that refreshing courtyard under the morning sun had any relationship either to the imagination or to a bitch in heat, though later I understood that this thought's intromission had to do with me and the sweet thing previously splayed open by torturers and nothing to do with the woman now walking down the corridor. Thereby was revealed to me conclusively the very image that had forced me to flee from the office where I had been working, focused as I was on correcting the report that contained the testimony of the girl raped over and over again, the image that had made my hair and my soul stand on end so intensely that I could not continue reading and the only thing I could think to do was flee to the courtyard to get some sunshine and fresh air to dispel that image, which of course did not happen, because sitting on the edge of the fountain, while Pilarica perorated about her problems with work, I again felt the shudder of that girl who walked with such difficulty through the basement of the police station, dragged along by Lieutenant Octavio Pérez, her vagina and anus torn to shreds, barely able to take a step and still unaware of the gonorrhea infection that was beginning to eat away at her and the putrid semen that was turning into a fetus in her uterus, paralyzed by terror, believing the lieutenant was leading her to the slaughterhouse, where they butchered the political prisoners and that is why she was but one single tremor of battered flesh as she entered the abattoir, where there was nothing but a prisoner hanging from the ceiling, naked, a Salvadoran guerrilla and arms dealer, the lieutenant explained to her, a mass of bloody, rotten, purulent flesh, where the worms had already made their appearance, for they had beaten him to a pulp, and he was barely able to utter a dull moan whereby the girl understood that *that* was still alive, an imperceptible moan that let the girl perceive a glimmer of consciousness in that dripping offal she stood, also naked, in front of, her hands tied behind her back and sheer terror in her eyes when the lieutenant grabbed her by the hair and forced her to move closer to the hanging body and told her, in the tone of voice of a scolding father, "that's what they're going to do to you if you don't cooperate," as if he had had nothing to do with the fists that had been beating her, the boots kicking her, the penises ripping through her vagina and anus, and the lieutenant signaled to the henchman in charge of the abattoir, who took out a small sickle and swiftly heated the blade over a burning ember until it was red hot then passed it to the lieutenant, who expertly with one slice cut the penis and testicles off the bloated body in front of the astonished eyes of the girl, the lieutenant made that perfect castrating cut, which produced a howl as if the victim had been fully conscious, the most horrendous howl the girl had ever heard, which would awaken her at night for the rest of her life, as she asserted in her testimony, the same howl that made me stampede out of the bishop's office to the courtyard where I now found myself with the Toledan, while the woman who had survived such barbarism—thanks to pressure exerted by her uncle, who was a colonel, she was set free, according to what she stated in the report—went through the door of one of the offices, without me daring to let myself be introduced to her because I planned to keep as far away from her as possible throughout my stay at the archbishop's palace.

It was Pilar herself who shook me out of my nightmare by asking how things had gone the night before, if I had had a good time with Fátima, all with a mischievous smile, probably enjoying how disappointed I had been upon discovering that her friend had a boyfriend, without suspecting that the disappointment might have even been comical if I hadn't woken up the way I had: in a stupor from the overdose of Lexotan and regretting that I had not been awake when Fátima got up and left the apartment and therefore couldn't ask her to forget everything that had happened the night before, to erase the tape and never speak about it with anybody, least of all her boyfriend, Jay Cee, a petition for silence lodged in my esophagus from the time I got out of bed until the moment I reached the archbishop's palace and started wandering around looking for Fátima in vain—because at some moment during the night she informed me that she would spend that day meeting her beloved boyfriend and packing up her belongings for the move—until I shut myself up in the bishop's office and focused my attention on the testimony of the woman I had just seen in the corridors, making me momentarily forget my anxiety about the consequences that might result from the night I had spent with Fátima, an anxiety that shot through me again because of the trick question I posed to Pilarica in front of the fountain. What kind of a guy is this Uruguayan soldier? I asked, trying to take the bull by the horns, for my nerves were in no state for any kind of subterfuge, and if I had to prepare myself for the worst it was better to know it once and for all. But I already suspected that the Toledan's response would be full of a lot of ingenuousness, for she thought Jay Cee was a great guy, the best thing that could have happened to Fátima, he had nothing in common with the local military men, those brutes, but was rather an educated guy, very well traveled, super nice, very cool, she said, I just had to meet him, she had no doubt that we would get along really well. Suddenly I felt my mouth get parched, I felt like pushing Pilarica so she'd fall backward into the fountain, her legs in the air, then dashing out of there without knowing where I was going, but instead I managed to barely mumble in a thick pasty voice that I had to get back to my office to continue copyediting the one thousand one hundred pages for time was running out.

Tormented by a sense of foreboding, without being able to concentrate as well as I would have liked, I remained for the rest of the morning shut up in the bishop's office editing the aforementioned report, from time to time copying unusual sentences into my little notebook, sentences that let my mind wander for a brief spell, but in one way or another all led me back to my urgency to find Fátima, to ask her to forget about the events of the previous night and abstain from recounting them to her Jay Cee, sentences like the one spoken by a man of the Mam ethnic group, whose parents and brothers the military had made disappear after the massacre, and who since then had been living in the deepest depression, the sentence that read, *But always so very tired I feel that I can't do anything!*, with all its sadness and desolation, made me realize that I couldn't do anything to communicate with Fátima, in spite of the insistent and futile calls I made to the apartment she shared with Pilar, the sentence *But always so very tired I feel that I can't do anything!* turned in my head into something similar to the anxiety I was feeling at not being able to do anything to prevent Fátima, after the welcoming romp in bed, from whispering as innocently as she could in the ear of Major Jay Cee Medina something like, "I've got a little surprise for you, my love," which he would respond to with the indolence of a warrior exhausted from the recently waged battle of love, without paying too much attention, until the girl with the fetid feet told him with a mixture of enthusiasm and complicity that she had also had a "parallel encounter," in fact the night before, with a colleague from the archbishop's palace, who was me, a declaration that would whip up the Uruguayan soldier into a precipitous bout of rage and produce a fear of equal intensity in me, your humble servant, so much so that I stood up and began to pace compulsively around the bishop's office, imagining the postcoital scene between Fátima and her recently arrived boyfriend, I began to pace and scratch the head of my penis through my pants, I walked back and forth in front of the desk like a caged monkey and rubbed the head of my penis, as if with this gesture I could get rid of the image of that pair of lovebirds and female treason, which perhaps at that very instant was turning that Jay Cee into a fiend ready to crush my bones, when in fact what was happening was that the whole morning I had been feeling a slight itching at the tip of my penis and a kind of tightness around my testicles, sensations which I'd attributed to irritation naturally produced by a sexual encounter after several weeks of abstinence, but that now, under sharper scrutiny, I noticed had gotten worse as the day wore on.

That from suspicion to panic not even a fraction of a second went by I can be absolutely certain by the speed at which I propelled myself out of the office and toward the bathrooms, by the state of mental turmoil I found myself suddenly engulfed in as I ran through the corridors, by the extreme emotional distress I felt as I entered the stall where, after locking the door, I proceeded to examine my member: I didn't need to squeeze it very hard to make a white drop appear, which left me dumbstruck, my mouth hanging open, as if I had been put under a spell, because never in my life had I had a venereal disease, because I believed I would never in my entire life catch such a disease, because what I had always most feared about carnal relations was the possibility of contracting a venereal disease. And no doubt whatsoever remained: the greatly feared drop of pus was there, looking at me accusatorily, while I had the sensation that the floor was collapsing under my feet, the vertigo of someone who has crossed a forbidden boundary, for until then I had believed that men were divided into two groups, the dirty and the virtuous, and it was precisely the possession of this drop or the lack thereof that constituted the line separating them.

That from panic to indignation I passed in a fury I am certain because before I had even left the stall and gotten to the sink, my fear that Fátima would recount her nocturnal adventures to her soldier lover had been expunged from my soul and instead my entire being became possessed with the idea of revenge, with the search for the best way to repay the dirty trick that little Spanish chick had played on me, for it was impossible that she was unaware that she was a carrier of the infection now eating away at me and that the Uruguayan soldier had undoubtedly infected her with, habitué of who knows what prostitutes, only the worst kind of treachery could lead her to rub her infection off on me the way she had and only my worst treachery could pay her back, I told myself as I splashed water on my face, as if in this way I could rid myself of the plague I had caught, without any desire at all to go back and shut myself up in the bishop's office unless it was to take immediate action against that diseased scoundrel, which is just what I would do, call my friend Erick and ask him to please recommend a urologist because one of his employees had infected me with a venereal disease, I would even ask Pilarica for a referral to a medical man to treat the disease that her compatriot had given me the night before, which I would explain to her in detail so that she would realize what kind of a friend she had and finally dispel that stupid little giggle. And I would even insinuate to the bishop that I wasn't making much progress on copyediting the report, nor working with the kind of focus I'd hoped for, and that the fault lay with that Fátima, who had disgraced me with her putrid cunt. But the powerful memory of that pearl of pus between my legs made me understand that this was an issue of first things coming first, that my strategy for repudiating Fátima could wait, and that first I had to stop the infection, so, swiftly, perhaps with the speed of one possessed, I made my way toward the enormous wooden door, crossed the filthy street teeming with beggars and street vendors, and entered the corner drugstore to find a pharmacist who could give me a prescription for the strongest possible penicillin to treat the disease I had caught.

TEN

I ARRIVED AT THE HOUSE at 1-25 Sexta Avenida sharply at eight-thirty, exactly as I had been instructed, for Pilarica had made it clear to me that this was when the birthday party for Johnny Silverman would begin, a New York Jew and a member of the team of forensic anthropologists working with the archdiocese, excavating sites of documented massacres to recover the bones of the victims in order to confirm the testimonies and allow the living to hold funeral services for the dead in keeping with the rituals and traditions of the indigenous cultures, even if it was many years later and nobody was able to distinguish precisely the bones of one from the bones of another, for the army had buried so many in mass graves. I arrived at Johnny Silverman's house at the appointed hour with no expectations other than to spend a relaxing evening, abstemious as I found myself due to the antibiotics I was taking to counteract the infection already discussed and which had been the cause of an altercation with Fátima that afternoon, for she categorically denied that either she or her boyfriend were infected with any disease and even dared insinuate that I was trying to slander her, so I proposed that she accompany me to the bishop's office at that very moment and I would show her the sinister drop in private, an invitation she turned down with some excuse or other while she went on sweetening her coffee in the kitchen of the archbishop's palace, where we were arguing in whispers, because it simply wasn't possible, I insisted, that the little drop appeared precisely the morning after she had taken advantage of me and that it just so happened that the carrier of this disease exhibited no symptoms whatsoever, a point that made her even more upset and led her to cut short the discussion, this wasn't the place for that kind of conversation, she said as she left. I entered Johnny Silverman's house and was surprised that the host himself opened the door, looking rather disheveled with a kitchen knife in his hand, and that the living room was empty as if the party had been cancelled, a suspicion I expressed at that very moment, but Johnny explained that the guests would start to arrive in a few minutes and that I was the first, besides Charlie, who was already in the kitchen helping him prepare some food, that he himself was running late because of something that had come up at work at the last minute, and he still hadn't even taken a much-needed shower, a point I agreed with him on, based on how dirty he looked. I couldn't help noticing, all the way from the front door to the kitchen, the large rooms in this beautiful colonial house and the excellent taste of its decor and furnishings, not in the same league as the apartment in the Engels Building where I spent my nights and that could by rights be considered a dump in comparison to this grandeur I still wasn't seeing to its full extent, an idea that led me to conclude through a series of associations that it was much more profitable to dig up Indians' bones than edit pages bearing their testimonies, though I must admit that Pilarica had told me that this Johnny Silverman belonged to a wealthy Jewish family from New York that owned a penthouse in Manhattan as well as many other properties, which somehow might explain the difference between his house and my apartment, but not something else I would soon begin to suspect. An olive-skinned beauty with long thick black locks greeted me with the insolence of a woman who knows many desire her and the richest one possesses her after Johnny said that this was Tania, his girlfriend, and the other was Charlie, a guy with a shaved head *a la* Yul Brynner, who immediately unsheathed his Argentinean accent. "Sorry, but I don't remember your name," Johnny said to me, for we had been introduced in my friend Erick's office and had never seen each other again, but he said it as coolly as he then turned back to his culinary labors assisted by Tania and Charlie, who were sitting at the table in the spacious kitchen cutting up sausages and arranging them on platters, he said it as lightheartedly as when afterward he asked me what I would like to drink, pointing to the table the bottles were set out on and then continuing his story about the excavations he was then carrying out on the outskirts of an abandoned military base in the Petén region, where they had found the bones of seventy-seven persons of all ages, including pregnant women and newborn babies, as Johnny specified. *For always the dreams they are there still,* I said as a kind of amen when Johnny finished his story, which created a certain discomfort among those present, especially the birthday boy, who perhaps thought my words were part of some foreign ritual he wasn't familiar with. *For always the dreams they are there still,* I repeated, a splendid sentence that had lit up my afternoon at the archbishop's palace, its sonority, its impeccable structure, which spread itself out into eternity without skipping over the moment, its use of the adverb to wring the neck of time, a sentence spoken in the testimony of an old indigenous woman from who knows which ethnic group and that could have been referring to the massacre whose bones the team of forensic anthropologists, of which Johnny was a member, were digging up, a sentence both luminous (due to its suggestion of possible meanings) and terrible (because it was in fact about the nightmare of terror and death). *For always the dreams they are there still*, I proclaimed for the third time, my eyebrows raised, on the verge of enthusiasm, so that they would understand once and for all its transcendence, so that the Argentinean shaved *a la* Yul Brynner would not again ask me if I wanted a drink, because I would follow up his question with the answer that I was taking antibiotics and was forbidden to drink alcohol, so that they could turn those recently dug-up bones into words, into poetry of the best kind, into something that wouldn't fit into the pea-sized brains I suspected they had as they exchanged suspicious glances, that these guys needed me to repeat once again and with a slightly different emphasis, *For always the dreams they are there still*, as I was willing to do, but at that moment a shrill screech rang out from the ceiling of the kitchen, the front doorbell, they said, just as the dark-skinned woman named Tania announced that she would get the door and Johnny Silverman started down the hallway to go take a shower, for it really was time he did so. "Hey, that great sentence," Yul Brynner asked, "where did you get it?" just as a peal of laughter and the sounds of people talking reached us from the living room, as if the guests had reached an agreement to all arrive at the same time. "Impressive, man. Sounds like a line from César Vallejo," said the Argentinean with a certainty that disconcerted me, I must admit, as if that person knew what I was thinking and I had already talked to him about it, a circumstance that from any point of view would have been impossible for it was the first time I had met that shaved guy, who, I soon found out, worked for the U.N. and was an old friend of Johnny's from when they both lived in New York, this guy with a shaved head who very cunningly segued from his remarks about Vallejo's poetry and its relationship to indigenous languages to a subtle interrogation about my work at the archdiocese and my friendship with Erick, all packaged neatly into his conversation with me at the kitchen table, not paying any attention to calls to join the group in the living room, where things were picking up, as if he were placing me inside a bubble constructed out of his crafty questions and my inevitable answers, as if the guy had known ahead of time about the psychological problems that afflicted me and that consisted of wanting to tell everything once I'd been encouraged to start talking, down to the hairs and the smells, spill it all out to a point of satiety, compulsively, in a kind of verbal spasm, as if it were an orgiastic race that would culminate in my total abandon, until I was left without secrets, until my interlocutor knew all he wanted to know, in an exhaustive confession after which I would suffer the worst possible backlash. And that's just what happened: I explained in detail about the one thousand one hundred pages, about my relationship with my friend Erick, about the Spanish hidalgo and the little guy with the Mexican mustache, about the memorable characters who swarmed around the archbishop's palace, like that woman dozens of times raped, or the Toledan suffering because her boyfriend had betrayed her, or the other Spanish girl who had given me an infection I was trying to combat and thus my abstinence. And then there was a click, as if some switch had been flipped, as if the enchanted bubble had popped, as if the mention of my ailment had been repulsive to the shaved Argentinean, who suddenly had an indecipherable expression on his face, an absence, that even made me feel sorry for him because perhaps I had reminded him of some similar contagion he had once contracted. It was then, in order to try to re-establish contact, even just by changing the subject, that I asked him if he was from Buenos Aires or the countryside. "I'm Uruguayan," he said between clenched teeth, with such an ugly look in his eyes that I managed only to ask where the bathroom was, stand up, and walk like a zombie past the other guests, with the sensation of falling into a dark, bottomless pit, because like a madman I had exposed my flanks to an astute enemy, who to Johnny was Charlie, but to his lover and other intimates was Jay Cee, Major Juan Carlos Medina, the soldier who was now hatching a plan with various options for annihilating me once I left the bathroom, because as long as I remained seated on the toilet with my guts tied up in knots of fear, he would be getting more and more incensed by the words that had senselessly poured out of my mouth, by the fact that the Spanish girl I had been talking about so disparagingly was to all appearances Fátima, although I never mentioned her name, because nobody knew better than he that the aforementioned disease had come from his own infected penis. Paralyzed, my mind gone blank, not knowing what to do, wishing that the whole thing had been some kind of nightmare from which I would soon awake, I discovered that Johnny's bathroom was luxury itself: the walls were covered with gorgeous tiles like in a Moorish palace, there was a wide bathtub one could frisk about in with two damsels, a large cedar wardrobe, several throw rugs, modern tools and implements probably for personal grooming, which I didn't even know existed, mirrors of various sizes that reflected my contrite face, a French window with frosted-glass panes . . . Then the knocks sounded on the door, imperious, urgent. "It's occupied," I managed to stammer as my gut contracted, knowing that it could only be Jay Cee, who had come to make sure I hadn't escaped and was standing by the bathroom door waiting for me to come out, where he would be able to trap me and pay me back for the horns that girl of his had perched on his head, perhaps treating me to a most humiliating beating in front of his cohorts if I came out, or dragging me out into the street with the most sinister of intentions, a possibility that sealed off my sphincter. Jay Cee banged on the door again with the same imperious urgency, which made me stand up like a shot and button up my pants, I flushed the toilet and started pacing around desperately, like a cornered rat, for that's what I felt like, until I stopped in front of the French window with frosted-glass panes, which I opened without difficulty and through which I stepped into a corridor around an internal courtyard, dark and smelling of vegetation I could barely make out, a corridor I moved along as cautiously as possible, a shadow among the shadows searching for a place where I could hide while I put my thoughts in order, alleviate my fear, and calm the agitation I was sweating out of every pore. Avoiding the large ceramic pots and a stair here or there, always hugging the walls of the corridor, watching for Jay Cee coming through the bathroom window, I reached the far end of the courtyard, where I then came to a hallway that led to another section of that colonial mansion and down which I scampered in the hopes of finding a door leading out to the street, because the only sensible thing was for me to hightail it out of there as soon as possible, but just then I heard steps and voices coming toward me, as if the cuckolded soldier had gotten together a posse and was setting up an ambush, so I had to quickly crouch down behind a large pot and wait for my pursuer to pass by me, which didn't happen, because none of the three guys who appeared in the hallway and entered a side door was the shaved guy I so feared, instead I recognized Johnny Silverman and my friend Erick, together with a third guy I had never seen in my life. The light they turned on in the room lit up the rear window located right next to the pot I was hiding behind, which left me in an optimal position to observe them sitting down around the table and placing a bottle of whisky on it, without them being aware of my presence thanks to the umbrageous plant growing in the pot and the darkness in the hallway, but without my being able to understand the murmurs they were conspiring in, as I soon ascertained, for the rear window allowed nothing else to filter out, just that unintelligible murmur. But even the deafest man on earth would have realized that these three men were exchanging secrets, confidential information, words forbidden for the uninitiated, which surprised me as far as my friend Erick was concerned, but which then led me to wonder what a rich New York Jew was doing digging up bones of indigenous people massacred by the army of a country where they would fry him alive for doing much less than that, and moreover what the hell was he doing conspiring with a representative of the Catholic Church, like my friend Erick, and with that other guy, who from any angle looked like a military man—upright bearing, harsh expression—in fact a high-ranking officer in civilian clothes undoubtedly a half-dozen bodyguards were waiting for outside, for my intuition never led me astray, especially not about his eyes, like those of a cobra about to attack, for a moment I was even afraid he had detected my presence behind that plant in the darkness. That was when the pathways in my mind came full circle: that intelligence officer could be none other than General Octavio Pérez Mena, the torturer of the girl of the archdiocese and the slayer of Indians, whose picture I had never seen because the sly fox knew how to remain invisible, living in the shadows was his specialty and the press couldn't get hold of him even in their dreams. Horrified, I wanted to get away from there so as not to witness a conspiracy that could cost me my life, but I had nowhere to retreat, for surely that Jay Cee was already snooping around the courtyard and any moment would come walking down this corridor, so it was better for me to remain quietly in my hiding place, alert to the shadows behind me and the cabal behind the glass, because if the shaved man with horns appeared I could in a flash burst into the room, where my friend Erick would defend me, where I could explain to him that due to a misunderstanding that guy wanted to trounce me, so those three would never suspect there'd been an eavesdropper at the rear window nor could Jay Cee act upon his rage. Speculating about the possible subject of their deliberations I was, trying to guess what their lips they were saying, when I felt behind me a presence, so close I didn't dare move a muscle, so devilishly close I could feel its breath upon my neck, as if the shaved one had knelt down stealthily behind me so he also could peak through the same window, so he could enjoy simultaneously the cabal behind the glass and the terror he was inspiring in me; in the face of this terror the testimony I'd corrected that afternoon popped into my head, *There are moments I have fear and even I start to shout*, which was exactly the one thing I wanted to do at that moment and the last thing I could do, out of fear begin to shout. But eternal seconds passed without there being a sign or a word, until there sounded in my ear that typical canine snuffle requesting attention or affection, which made me very cautiously turn my head to see a mastiff puppy, friendly, with a split lip, as if he had a harelip, eager to play right then and there, probably the poor thing wasn't allowed inside where the guests were dancing, and once he knew he had my attention he started frisking about, frisking up and down the hallway, barking playfully, which immediately raised the alarm for the trio conspiring in the room, which gave me no choice but to quickly return to the hallway and escape through the shadows, not caring if I fell into the clutches of the shaved Argentinean, for I was much more afraid of being trapped by General Octavio Pérez Mena, who would proceed to interrogate me mercilessly about why I was spying on them, using his most expeditious method of beating me to soften me up, then taking me to his macabre abattoir, but thank God the mastiff caught the scent of his owner, because his loud playful barks continued down the hallway as I moved toward the bathroom window I had climbed through, which was now closed, which meant I had to continue straight until I got to the living room full of guests, which I stumbled my way through to prevent the aforementioned general from running up behind me without my noticing, right on my heels. I was trying to get to the front door when I unexpectedly bumped into the shaved one and Fátima—*damn!*—that was all I needed, stuck between a rock and a hard place, the merciless slayer at my heels and the cuckold and his girlfriend in front of me. “Where did you go?” she asked, with the innocence of a young lady at her first holy communion, while I awaited a trouncing by the shaved one. “You already met Charlie,” she continued as I tried to make my way out. “What the hell is going on with you? Man, you look like you’ve seen a ghost,” she said, taking me by the arm as I turned around so as not to see the face of the shaved one who was hugging her. “Too bad Jay Cee couldn’t make it. I would have loved for you to meet him,” I heard her say, and then she explained that Charlie was one of Jay Cee’s best friends, a compatriot and colleague, she specified, without her explanation managing to detain me from fleeing into the street.

ELEVEN

AS IF FREE OF FEAR I AWOKE that first morning in my assigned room at the spiritual retreat center, where they had brought me the previous day, my friend Erick and a chauffeur from the archdiocese, so I could focus intensely for no longer than ten days on the final revisions of the one thousand one hundred pages so they could be sent as soon as possible to the printer, because I had been the one to tell my friend Erick of my need to shut myself away to work someplace far from worldly cares, someplace where I could focus twenty-four hours a day without any interruptions on the job I had been hired to do, for otherwise I would not be able to guarantee that the report had been revised with the necessary care, as I told Erick a few days before my removal to this spiritual retreat center located in a forested area on the outskirts of the city, a large modern building comprised of forty identical rooms in the shape of a cross and with a common space in the middle where the kitchen, the vast dining room, a library, and a small chapel were located.

As if free of nightmares I awoke that first morning in that austere room with white walls, lying in my bunk where I enjoyed contemplating, through the glass door that faced the large lawn and the pine forest beyond, the fog drifting by on the breeze, as if suddenly I had woken up in a different country where nature had made of man a less bloodthirsty creature, a feeling that evoked my old aspirations of living life in a different way with my mind and my emotions infused with fresh air and positive vibrations, so much so that I immediately got out of bed and donned my exercise outfit, my sweatpants and tennis shoes, for I had only to slide open the glass door to go out and jog and thus reinvent myself, which is what I did—*gracious me!*—the untamed and humid air impregnated my lungs with newfound enthusiasm as I ran across the lawn surrounding the building shaped like a cross, my mind focused on the occurrence of my breath and on my muscles, all of which were performing in a satisfactory way despite the fact that I had done no physical exercise for several months. By the time I finished my first lap around the spiritual retreat center I had verified that there were no other residents, as my friend Erick had anticipated, who told me that during the week I would be alone with the administrative and service staff, such as that gardener I could see near the forest, but that on Saturdays and Sundays the house would be swarming with catechists, a situation that pleased me on the one hand because there would be nothing to interrupt me during my work days, but on the other hand made me slightly uneasy, considering that if a determined enemy wanted to destroy me and the aforementioned report they would not have the least difficulty penetrating the forest surrounding us, arriving nonchalantly at the sliding-glass door of my room, and proceeding to destroy both of us, a thought that dampened the high spirits with which I began my second lap around the house of retreat and which resulted in my failing to enjoy the clean air and the landscape, I even lost the rhythm of my breathing I had so successfully achieved, burying me under old fears, the dense forest ceased to be a cause for celebration and became the sight of an ambush, and now there was no more jogging to cleanse my body and spirit but rather a wild dash to the room I would be shut up in for so many hours throughout the coming days, staring at the computer screen that we had brought from the bishop's office and that sat on the small table next to the sliding-glass door, the table where I sat as it grew dark and where I began to watch with a good dose of fear the dense foliage of the forest, until I chose to rush down the deserted hallway to the dining room, where I would eat dinner alone, chewing over those parts of the report that had made an impact on me, like the testimony that said, *At first I wished to have been a poisonous snake, but now what I ask for is their repenting,* which impressed me particularly for the fact that someone would want to be a poisonous snake, that an indigenous person would believe that he could become a poisonous snake in order to take his revenge, and it impressed me so much that that night I abstained from opening the glass door for fear that a snake from the forest would come slithering across the grass and, taking advantage of my carelessness, swiftly infiltrate my room, a fear that made me remember General Octavio Pérez Mena's mug, like that of a poisonous snake, when I saw him talking with Johnny the Jew and my friend Erick, whom, by the way, I never asked about what I had witnessed through the rear window, for my curiosity grew mute in the face of my fear, as could be seen from that night at the spiritual retreat center when I not only refrained from opening the sliding-glass door but also closed the blinds so as to completely separate myself from the dark lawn where I would have suddenly seen General Octavio Pérez Mena's face like that of a poisonous snake, his sinister countenance pushing up against the glass door—*shit!*—I would flee in a panic, howling down the silent hallways in search of the guard's hut, even though it would be an effort in vain, of course, for by the time the torturer's countenance would have appeared at my glass door, the room would already be surrounded by a commando unit.

That solitude can break even the halest of spirits I was able to ascertain after my third day of seclusion at the spiritual retreat center, after spending hour upon hour saying not a word to anybody, exchanging greetings only at meal times with the staff, deeply immersed in copyediting the report, sleeping fitfully in that small bunk, lacking even the most minimum of pleasures, for I wasn't even granted the relief of jacking off due to the disease afflicting me (though there were no longer any drops coming out of my penis), thus my mind began to become so perturbed that the same image kept asserting itself whenever I took a break, an image that recurred several times in the report and that little by little invaded me until it had taken complete possession of me, at which point I stood up and began to pace around the small space of my room, between the desk and the bunk, like one possessed, as if I were that lieutenant who had brutally burst into the hut of that indigenous family, grabbed in my iron hand by the heel that baby only a few months old, raised it over my head and begun to swing it around through the air, faster and faster, as if it were David's sling from which a rock would be launched, swinging it around at a dizzying speed under the horrified gaze of the parents and siblings until the baby's head suddenly crashed against a beam inside the hut, exploding, the brains spraying out everywhere, I swung it in the air by the heels until I came back to my senses and I noticed that I had been about to bash my arm, which I had been swinging violently over my head, against the headrest of my bunk because I wasn't in a hut but rather in my small room at the spiritual retreat center, nor was I that lieutenant who busted the heads of newborn babies against beams in the middle of a massacre, but rather a copyeditor distressed by the perusal of this testimony several times repeated in the report. Then, in a sweat and with my nerves on edge, I sat back down in front of the computer, forcing myself to make progress on the text, for time was of the essence, I persevered at my work obsessively until a few hours later when my concentration languished and once more I became possessed by that same image, I stood up, I became Lieutenant Octavio Pérez Mena, the official in charge of the unit assigned to the massacre, I returned to the hut of those fucking Indians who would understand the hell that awaited them only when they saw flying through the air the baby I held by the ankles so I could smash its head of tender flesh against the wood beam. And it was the splattering of palpitating brains that brought me back to my senses: I found myself in the middle of the room, shaking, sweating, a little dizzy because of the vertiginous movements of swinging the baby over my head, but at the same time with a feeling of lightness, as if I had taken a load off my back, as if my transformation into the lieutenant who exploded the heads of newborn babies against beams had been a catharsis, freeing me from the pain accumulated over the one thousand one hundred pages, which I soon dug into again, in a repetitive cycle of prolonged concentration broken by intervals of the same macabre fantasy.

But on the fourth day, I have to admit it, my mind went out of control and I no longer had any moments of relief, the barbarities I read about again and again—while searching for the last misplaced comma, the astute slip of the tongue, or the slightly unclear sentence, because at this point it would have been insane to delve into revisions of the actual content—were sinking in so deeply that by then I was beside myself, and when my eyes were not following the text on the screen it was my mind that was transported to the theater of events and then it was no longer mine, if it ever had been, but rather wandered, of its own free will, like a journalist, around the village commons, where the soldiers, machetes in hand, chopped up the bound and kneeling residents; or it entered a hut where the brains of the baby were flying through the air; or it descended into the mass grave among the mutilated bodies—as if the bellyful I had read had not been enough; my mind had to wander through a vicious circle of images that by midnight were disturbing me so much that I just barely managed to slide open the glass door to step out onto the cold dark patio and howl like a sick animal under the star-studded sky, I opened the sliding-glass door and went outside to howl on the wind-blown patio without thinking that a poisonous snake could be lying in wait for me, without considering that General Octavio Pérez Mena with his posse of hired assassins could get hold of me, I let out three howls that were so loud the guard must have thought it was a coyote. But then, when I came back to my senses and collected myself after such excessive behavior, still standing in the middle of the patio in the dark and the buzzing wind, I perceived shadows discreetly approaching from both sides of the patio, four shadows that very soon would be silhouettes and would have me surrounded—*damn it!*—under the circumstances any move to return to my room would have been suicidal, so I quickly ran toward the deep darkness of the forest in such a sudden and unexpected flight that my pursuers had no time to react, thus I slipped away, espying the path through the pine trees and the undergrowth I had followed during my morning jogs, a path I followed now in the dark, my heart pounding as hard as it could, afraid that they would catch up to me, start shooting toward where I was running and out of breath, or that other henchmen were posted along the path to trap me; but at a particular moment my mind cleared, as if fear had opened the doors of perception, that's how I felt, crossing the forest along that path amid the humid scents and the sounds of my own fear, finding my way as if I had always known it, without bumping up against a tree or suffering a fatal fall, just tripping slightly once or twice, always with the sensation of having escaped along that path before, as if I were living the same thing again and with the certainty that my pursuers had chosen to let me escape and then turned back to my room, where they would proceed to confiscate the report, or even destroy the computer and the diskettes, confident that thereby they would prevent its publication, as I continued along that path that would soon lead me to some pastures beyond which I would find the main highway to the city, if my sense of direction hadn't failed me, because I amazed myself, how well I could see in the dark. I hadn't erred: after following a fence line I came out on the highway and turned and ran along it, listening for the sound of a vehicle, for those men who had surrounded me on the patio would have to drive by this very spot, probably looking for me where there wouldn't be any witnesses, so every time a vehicle approached I crouched down along the edge of the highway, behind a tree trunk or a stone wall, and then took off running again when I heard the motor fading away in the distance.

And to the cadence of my running footfalls my fickle memory kept me keep repeating between clenched teeth the last sentence I had chosen that night for my notebook, a sentence that at first glance didn't appear to be anything extraordinary, but in the velocity of my flight took on the cadence of those tunes warriors chant to fire themselves up as they march, the sentence, *Wounded, yes, is hard to be left, but dead is ever peaceful,* became a war cry I sang as I jogged down the road, a sentence that came to my mind perhaps because it fit so perfectly with the cadence of a forced march, so that soon I found myself singing out loud, *Wounded, yes, is hard to be left, but dead is ever peaceful,* not caring that due to my fervor I would fail to hear the approach of a vehicle with my pursuers but rather on the contrary it didn't take me long to find the right cause to infuse my song with belligerence and that could only have been the idea of returning to the spiritual retreat center to face the assault General Octavio Pérez Mena's commandos were waging against the memories and work of so many people, an idea that lit the wick of my enthusiasm as I was jogging down the highway, but right away exposed itself for all its senselessness when I heard a powerful engine approaching and immediately leaped off the road, terrified at the possibility that those criminals had seen me and would proceed to eliminate me, as it was senseless also for me to fervently chant the sentence, *Wounded, yes, is hard to be left, but dead is ever peaceful,* for that belonged to the sorrow of an indigenous woman who had survived the massacre and not to a copyeditor who was jogging precisely to avoid being left either wounded or dead.

I approached the first houses in the Mixco neighborhood and reviewed my options for defensive action, which were few, truth be told, and to be honest was barely one, because not for anything in the world would I have returned to my apartment in the Engels Building nor to Pilarica's, for those who wanted to destroy the report would have the lowdown on everybody working on it, not in vain did they call themselves the military intelligence service, and if they had dared to make an incursion into the church's spiritual retreat center with total impunity they would strike me down at the Toledan's house. The only thing left for me to do was call my buddy Toto, who would in alarm pick up the phone and hear my plea for help, that it was urgent for him to come and get me without delay at the coordinates I proceeded to give him, emphasizing that the hit men were on the prowl. Then I crouched down behind a garbage can near the public telephone booth to wait for my buddy to appear, for this was the only place I could hide where neither my pursuers nor a night watchman would find me, and while I was hiding and trembling I was racked by guilt for having abandoned my post, imagining what the bishop or my friend Erick might think about my disappearance and if they might not assume some collusion on my part, a thought I defended myself against by recalling the suspicious meeting between my friend Erick, General Octavio Pérez Mena, and Johnny the Jew, because this wasn't an issue of someone pointing a finger, and my concern that they would lose the hundreds of testimonies of so many survivors didn't make sense, for there would undoubtedly be copies of the report on the computers of my friend Erick, the gallant Joseba, and the little guy with the Mexican mustache, and as if this weren't enough, I took out of my leather jacket my little notebook, for I never went anywhere without it and my passport, to look for fragments of the testimony I had copied down in the last few days, which in that pestilent shadow behind the garbage can I just barely managed to see so as to make my wait more tolerable, a text that said, *May they wipe out the names of the dead to make them free, then no more problems we'll have,* which made it clear that even some of the indigenous survivors didn't want to recover memories but rather perpetuate forgetting.

With joy I leapt out of my hiding place half an hour later when I heard my buddy Toto's car stop, and the door had not even closed behind me when I blurted out the story of the assault on the patio at the retreat center, the thugs' siege, and my timely reaction, with so many fits and starts that my buddy Toto thought it wise to tell me only to calm down, as if I would have been able to tell it calmly when what I wanted to communicate were my suspicions that the assault I had just escaped from unharmed by the skin of my teeth could have been related to the conspiracy I had witnessed through the rear window. "Want to go back and see what has happened?" my buddy Toto asked me, concerned but with firmness. I answered him, not a chance, I had already considered that possibility during my escape, but the risk was too high, it would be better for him to put me up and in the morning he could give me a hand, because the army didn't know who he was and he could go to my apartment in the Engels Building to remove my few belongings and the money hidden in a secret nook of the closet, which I would use to buy a plane ticket to go away as far as possible. "Let's take a look. We've got nothing to lose," my buddy Toto insisted, to my surprise.

TWELVE

PLANET EARTH DOESN'T WANT TO KNOW anything nor does she understand what the comet tells her, for she is happy in her orbit and hates to be disturbed by someone who appears only every once in a while from who knows where, I thought that day at dawn while leaning on the bar at Peter's, staring into the mirror where I saw my face reflected over a row of bottles, where in fact dozens of drinkers next to me and behind me were reflected, through the dense cigarette smoke and the enthusiastic voices of those who were initiating the longest bacchanalia of the year, their so-called Carnival—which has nothing to do with what I call by that name—drinkers enthusiastically offering toasts and whom I could barely make out in the well-lit room, for my attention was focused on my own face reflected in the mirror, concentrating as I was on each and every one of my features, on the expression on my face, which suddenly looked different to me, as if he who was there wasn't me, as if that face for an instant were somebody else's, a stranger's, and not my everyday face, an instant when I was unrecognizable to myself and that caused me to panic, such extreme panic that I feared a bout of insanity among those strangers in a strange city if Cousin Quique hadn't just then appeared alongside me, because nobody likes to look at himself in the mirror and find somebody else. "Those two faggots are blowing each other in the bathroom," Cousin Quique complained as he settled in at the bar. "I wanted to go take a shit and those two assholes didn't get out of the bathroom because they were sucking each other's cocks," Cousin Quique repeated with his hallmark vulgarity. I asked him how he could be sure without having seen anything, and he responded that he had clearly heard them making comments about the fellatio they were performing, for Cousin Quique spoke German fluently and his anger convinced me that he couldn't possibly be lying. I suggested that maybe the native custom was to perform fellatio at the beginning of so-called Carnival, for all peoples have their customs and practices, I said, and if they called that parade of floats at four in the morning when the temperature was twenty degrees Fahrenheit Carnival, I wouldn't be at all surprised if instead of dancing half naked, like at the carnivals I was used to, they chose to perform fellatio in a nice warm bathroom. But Cousin Quique still wasn't paying attention to me but instead was ordering another beer from Peter and striking up a conversation with a pale girl standing next to him, a good-looking Dutch girl he wanted to get into bed, for women were his obsession and his weakness, so once again I was left drinking alone in the throng, clutching my mug, fearful of encountering my unfamiliar face in the mirror, thinking that I was the comet and Cousin Quique Planet Earth, which was why he seemed so bored when I tried to explain to him my experiences copyediting those one thousand one hundred pages, because for him it concerned a remote galaxy that he no longer had anything to do with and his only response was to scold me for not having included in my contract with the church the cost of treatment to cure me of the psychological and emotional trauma I was subjected to while reading over and over again the aforementioned report, and perhaps he was right, for in spite of finding myself on the other side of the world, a morbid state of melancholy prevented me from enjoying the peace around me, and at Cousin Quique's slightest provocation I would bring up the corrected text and the experience I'd had a few weeks before, not yet lost my habit of pulling out my small notebook to read those sentences that moved me so much, many of which I already knew by heart, like the one that said, *For me remembering, it feels I am living it once more*, whose broken syntax was the corroboration that something had snapped in the psyche of the survivor who said it, a sentence that fully applied to my situation in this foreign and distant city where I had taken refuge thanks to Cousin Quique's hospitality, where for me remembering was living once more the nightmarish testimonies read so many times. "Would you like another beer?" Peter asked me, the simpatico Swiss giant, owner of the tavern, the only one in the whole place who spoke Spanish, moving quickly back and forth behind the bar because there were so many customers, all desperately thirsty, and he placed in front of me the new mug overflowing with foam while I contemplated the street through the large plate-glass windows, still surprised by the hundreds of inhabitants who, ignoring the freezing inclement weather, swirled around in costumes on the dark sidewalks, enjoying themselves, applauding the floats as they passed by, and dancing to the sounds of drums and piccolos, as if they were in a witches' Sabbath from the Middle Ages. "Everything okay?" Peter asked me, perhaps upset by the sneer on my face in the midst of so much hullabaloo, to which I answered yes, such an elaborate carnival seemed incredible to me at dawn and during the worst possible winter, that my lack of knowledge of the language was a pity, for it prevented me from understanding the meaning of the floats and the jokes being made. But seconds later he was already at the other end of the bar and I remained once again facing my own face in the mirror, convinced that nothing bad would happen and that if I just stared hard enough at my eyes

I would discover something or at least conjure up the possibility of finding somebody instead of myself, and as a result of certain associations and the fear of discovering myself to be different in the mirror, there settled into my mind the sentence that said, *They were people just like us we were afraid of,* which I repeated without taking my eyes off myself, even when I lifted the beer mug I didn't lose sight of myself out of the corner of my eye nor did I stop repeating, *They were people just like us we were afraid of,* perhaps with so much emphasis that right away I felt Cousin Quique's hand on my shoulder, I saw his reflection approaching me in the mirror and asking me in my ear what was happening to me, if I was talking to him, to which I responded, turning around to look him in the eyes, *They were people just like us we were afraid of,* which of course unnerved him, as always when I responded with the sentence of an indigenous person who had escaped from death by the skin of his teeth, and then irritated him because of what he termed "my sick obsession," but that didn't happen now, him getting irritated, I mean, but instead Cousin Quique asked me what I was talking about, truly concerned, as if he feared an unpredictable and violent outburst, so I explained that the army had forced one half of the village's population to kill the other half, better for Indians to kill Indians and leave the living as marked men. "Let's go outside now, the floats I was telling you about are about to pass by," said Cousin Quique hurriedly, for he became quite uneasy every time I talked to him about politics or the army. "And the Dutch girl?" I asked him. "She's coming with us," he said, taking me by the arm and leading me toward the rack where the coats were hanging. But when I opened the door, the cold struck me so violently I told Cousin Quique that I wouldn't go out for anything in the world, that he shouldn't worry about me, I would stay nice and warm in the bar until we went home, he should go ahead and make a good impression on the Dutch girl so he could screw her afterward. And so it came to pass: I stayed behind slowly drinking my huge mug of beer, having one or another exchange with Peter, eluding the mirror, until I unavoidably took out my little notebook, for no specific reason, like the addict who lights another cigarette with the butt of the previous one or the loner who reads the newspaper at the bar, thus I leafed through my notebook and savored the sentences, repeating some out loud so I could enjoy their musicality and recall specific emotions, until Peter came back to ask me what I was reading at the precise moment I muttered the phrase that said, *The more they killed, the higher they rose up*, which in fact was a lament about the compensation awarded for one's neighbor's criminality, and which I pronounced in my most expressive voice to Peter's astonishment, for he didn't understand anything and I had to explain that the sentence synthesized the fact that in the society I came from, crime constituted the most efficient means of social climbing, thus *The more they killed, the higher they rose up*, I repeated, without an audience, for the Swiss giant had moved on to another customer. That was when I remembered that by that time there would be news about the report's publication, and I felt intense eagerness to find out what had happened the morning of the day before at the cathedral, where the bishop made the announcement with great fanfare, according to what my buddy Toto had told me by email, in the same email that informed me about his meeting with my friend Erick, who had expressed his upset at my sudden disappearance, as if I should have given explanations to somebody who was conspiring in the most suspicious way, as if that conspiracy wasn't to blame for my shivering from cold in a foreign city on the other side of the world, abandoned in a bar where I couldn't talk to anybody, only wishing to go back to Cousin Quique's apartment and turn on the computer and find out at least the title they had finally given the report, for I had suggested as a title one of the most powerful sentences found in the testimonies, the sentence that said, *We all know who are the assassins,* for me the most propitious, the right one to be the title of the report that really wanted to say precisely this, that *We all know who are the assassins,* a sentence I suggested at the last meeting convened by my friend Erick and the little guy with the Mexican mustache before going to cloister myself in the spiritual retreat center and that they listened to but didn't feel as enthusiastic about as I did. *"We all know who are the assassins!"* I exclaimed, lifting my arm to get Peter's attention, for I would now pay for my beers and make my way to Cousin Quique's apartment without waiting for him to return to the bar, for with the Dutch girl at his side there was no way to guarantee such a return. And that's what I was doing, waiting for Peter to bring me the check, when all of a sudden I realized to my amazement that leaning against the bar to my right and drinking was General Octavio Pérez Mena himself—*shit!*—the very same face I had seen through the rear window was now looking at me insolently through the mirror and when I responded with a threatening scowl, for the beers I'd drunk were many and his impunity here nonexistent, he turned away to avoid me, that sissy, which only added fuel to my ire and gave me the courage to shout at him, raising my mug in the air, *We all know who are the assassins!* for this was the toast that torturer deserved, to which he responded with the foolish smile of someone who doesn't understand the language he is being addressed in, as if in this way he could throw me off track, what a fool he must have thought me, so as soon as I paid Peter for what I had consumed, I turned toward the spy and spat right in his face: *Thereafter we live the time of distress*, to see how he'd respond, I spat out that sentence from the report that had been racing around in my head for the last few days and in response to which he gave me his most confounded smile and then said something in German, which of course I didn't understand and that surely was some pretext for putting me off, to which I repeated, already beside myself, *Thereafter we live the time of distress*, which was for me a kind of challenge that he took without paying any attention to me, addressing himself to Peter in a language beyond my comprehension.

Soon I was in the street, shivering, making my way through the crowd toward the Aschenplatz, where I would have to take the tram, for the streets downtown were closed to traffic because of the parades and celebrations; and to liven up my spirits in that multitude of strangers who were drinking and singing in the freezing dawn, and to chase away from my mind the ghost I had left behind in the bar, I shouted again and again at the top of my lungs, *We all know who are the assassins!*, a shout that fired up my passions and went wholly unnoticed in the midst of the hubbub of so-called Carnival, a shout I didn't stop shouting even in the tram full of revelers, but that I couldn't utter upon entering Cousin Quique's apartment, as had been my intention, because a loud moan stopped me in my tracks, the moans of the Dutch girl who was taking it all in with her legs flung wide apart, man, the alcohol evaporated from my blood in an instant when I saw that, and I was forced to move with the utmost caution so that my presence wouldn't undermine those moans that had a relatively high timbre, to tell the truth, for I felt them reverberating in my ear, even though I was shut up in the office where I slept, and that if I hadn't been intent on turning on the computer to check my email would soon have allowed me to jack off with the greatest ease. And, in fact, there in my inbox was a message from my buddy Toto, which I proceeded to open with the utmost eagerness, and which wasn't a letter so much as a kind of telegram that said, "Yesterday at noon the bishop presented the report in a bombastic ceremony in the cathedral; last night he was assassinated at the parish house, they smashed his head in with a brick. Everybody's fucked. Be grateful you left."